"Dave caught at the knife-wrist."

Dave Darrin on Mediterranean Service

OR

With Dan Dalzell on European Duty

By

H. IRVING HANCOCK

Author of "Dave Darrin at Vera Cruz," "Dave Darrin's
South American Cruise," The West Point Series,
The Annapolis Series, The Boys of the
Army Series, Etc., etc.

Illustrated

WILDSIDE PRESS

CONTENTS

CONTENTS

10   CONTENTS

DAVE DARRIN

ON MEDITERRANEAN SERVICE

CHAPTER I

GREEN HAT, THE TROUBLE-STARTER

"DAN," whispered Dave Darrin, Ensign, United States Navy, to his chum and brother officer, "do you see that fellow with the green Alpine hat and the green vest?"

"Yes," nodded Dan Dalzell.

"Watch him."

"Why?"

"He's a powerful brute, and it looks as though he's spoiling for a fight."

"You are not going to oblige him, are you?" asked Dalzell in a whisper, betraying surprise.

"Nothing like it," Darrin responded disgustedly. "Danny Grin, don't you credit me with more sense than that? Do you imagine I'd engage in a fight in a place like this?"

"Then why are you interested in what the fellow might do?" demanded Ensign Dan.

11

"Because I think there is going to be a lively time here. That fellow under the Alpine hat is equal to at least four of these spindling Spanish waiters. There is going to be trouble within four minutes, or I'm a poor guesser."

"Just let Mr. Green Hat start something," chuckled Ensign Dalzell in an undertone. "There are plenty of stalwart British soldiers here, and 'Tommy Atkins' never has been known to be averse to a good fair fight. The soldiers will wipe up the floor with him. Then there is the provost guard, patrolling the streets of Gibraltar. If Mr. Green Hat grows too noisy the provost guard will gather him in."

"And might also gather us in, if the provost officer thought us intelligent witnesses," muttered Darrin.

"That would be all right, too," grinned Dan. "There is bound to be a British army officer in command of the provost guard. As soon as we handed him cards showing us to be American naval officers he'd raise his cap to us, and that would be the end of it."

"I don't like to be present at rows in a place of this kind," Ensign Darrin insisted.

"Then we'd better be going," proposed Ensign Dalzell.

The place was Gibraltar, and the time nine o'clock in the evening. The two friends were seated well back in one of the several Spanish vaudeville theatres that flourish more or less in the city on the Great Rock, even in such times as this period of the great European War.

The theatre was not a low place, or it would not have been permitted to exist in Gibraltar, which, even in peace times, is under the strictest military rule, made much more strict at the beginning of the great war. The performance was an ordinary one and rather dull. At the moment three Spanish women occupied the stage, going rather hopelessly through the steps of an aimless dance, while three musicians ground out the music for the dancers. The next number, as announced on a card that hung at one side of the stage, was to be a pantomime.

One particularly unpleasant feature only was to be noted in the place. Wines and liquors were served to those who chose to order them, Spanish waiters passing up and down the aisles in search of custom.

Mr. Green Hat, to the knowledge of Ensigns Darrin and Dalzell, had been a much too frequent customer. He was now arguing with two waiters about an alleged mistake in the changing of the money he had handed one of them. From angry remonstrance Mr. Green Hat was now resorting to abusive language.

"I'd like to implant a wallop under that

rowdy's chin," muttered Dan Dalzell, as he started to rise.

"Don't try it," warned Ensign Dave, as he, too, rose.

Just then the lightning struck; the storm broke.

With an angry bellow, Mr. Green Hat leaped to his feet, knocking down one of the waiters. Four others rushed to the spot. The five promptly assailed Mr. Green Hat, and were swiftly reinforced by the one who had been floored.

But the stalwart, active brawler proved to be too much for the combined force of the waiters. As if they had been so many reeds, Mr. Green Hat brushed them aside with his fists .

"Grab the bloomin' rotter and throw 'im h'out!" bellowed a "Tommy Atkins," as the British soldier is collectively known.

A new note, in a decidedly American tone of protest, rose above the uproar.

"How dare you? What do you mean, fellow?" demanded a young man in a gray traveling suit, glaring up from the floor, to which he, an unoffending occupant of an aisle seat, had suddenly been hurled.

It was too much for Dan Dalzell, who promptly attempted to seize Mr. Green Hat as that individual, with the momentum of a steam roller, rushed up the aisle.

Dalzell reached out a hand to grip Mr. Green

Hat by the collar. All too promptly a heavy fist smote Dan in the chest, knocking him back into the arms of Dave Darrin. Dave himself could not act quickly enough to avenge the blow that had been dealt his chum, because Dan's body blocked the way.

Four or five British soldiers at the rear of the little theatre tried to intercept Mr. Green Hat as he dashed up the aisle. Three of the "Messrs. Atkins" went to the floor, under the seats, while the others were brushed aside, and Mr. Green Hat reached the street.

"Stop that thief!" roared the young man in the gray suit. "He has robbed me!"

By this time Dalzell was again on his feet and out in the aisle. He sprinted for the street, followed closely by Dave Darrin. The young man in the gray suit, his face pallid, plunged after the young naval officers.

"You're an American, aren't you?" called Dave, over his shoulder.

"Yes," answered he of the gray suit, "and in official life at Washington, too. That scoundrel has robbed me of something of value to the United States government."

That was enough for Darrin and Dalzell. Though the charge might prove to be false, it was enough to cancel Dave's scruples against fighting.

Out into the street ahead of them ran a waiter, who had taken no part in the scrimmage, waving his arms and shouting:

"*Esta dirección!*" ("This way!")

"*Sigue andando!*" ("Keep right on!") roared Danny Grin, darting down the street at a hard pace.

But a moment later both naval officers, followed by the young man in gray and the waiter, came to a halt, for, directly ahead of them, on the well-lighted street, suddenly appeared a patrol detachment of the British provost guard.

"Did you stop the fellow who ran this way, sir?" hailed Ensign Darrin, as he recognized the uniform of the British infantry officer in command of the detachment.

"We didn't see any man running this way," replied the British lieutenant, smartly returning the salute that Ensign Darrin had given him.

"Didn't *see* any fellow running?" repeated three Americans, in tones of bewilderment.

"We were chasing a thief, sir," Darrin continued, "and this waiter told us that the fugitive ran this way."

"I — I thought he did," stammered the waiter in Spanish, though it was now plain that he understood English.

In deep disgust and with dawning suspicion, Dave Darrin glared at the waiter until that

fellow changed color and trembled slightly. Dave
was now certain that the waiter, probably by
previous arrangement, had shielded the escape of
Mr. Green Hat.

Turning to the English officer, Dave quickly
recounted what had happened. At the same
time he introduced himself and Dan as American
naval officers, and both tendered their cards.

"And you, sir? Who are you, and what did
you lose?" inquired the British officer, turning
to the young man in the gray suit.

"May I answer that question to an officer of
my own country?" appealed the young man in
the gray suit.

"Yes," assented the British officer, after keenly
regarding the stranger who claimed to have been
robbed.

"Will you step a few yards down the street
with me?" urged the unknown American, addressing Dave.

"Certainly," Darrin nodded, for he saw in-
sistent appeal in the stranger's gaze.

"Mr. Darrin," began the stranger, using the
name he had heard Dave announce in the intro-
ductions to the Britisher, "do you really belong
to the American Navy?"

"I do, indeed," Darrin answered. "I am at-
tached to the battleship 'Hudson,' now lying in
this harbor."

"Then I will introduce myself," continued the young man in the gray suit. "My name is George Cushing. Do you recognize the meaning of this?"

"This" proved to be a small gold badge, revealed by Cushing as he turned back the lapel of his coat. It was a badge worn by men belonging to a special branch of the secret service of the American Department of State. The members of this special service are usually found, if found at all, on duty in foreign countries.

"I know the badge, Mr. Cushing," nodded Dave Darrin. "Now, what have you to tell me?"

"That big man with the green hat must have started that fight with the waiters in the theatre to cover his intended attack on me," Cushing replied. "At the moment of knocking me down, he snatched from my coat pocket and made off with a most important document."

"Then you almost deserved to lose it, sir," replied Darrin sternly, "as a punishment for wasting your time in such a place as that theatre."

"I must see the American admiral as soon as possible," urged Cushing, ignoring Darrin's reproof. "But first of all, I must ask you to pass me safely by that provost guard, or I might be detained at a time when I cannot afford to lose a single instant. You will vouch for me, won't you, Mr. Darrin? Here are my formal credentials," continued Cushing, producing and unfolding a wallet that contained properly sealed and signed credentials from the American Department of State.

"The paper that was stolen from you did not in any way relate to the defenses and fortifications here at Gibraltar, did it?" Dave asked.

"Not in the least," Cushing replied promptly.

"You give me your word of honor for that?" Dave asked bluntly.

"Do you believe I'd waste my time on such rubbish as that?" demanded Cushing, scornfully. "Why, every civilized government on earth possesses accurate plans of the fortifications at Gibraltar! I give you my word of honor, Mr. Darrin, that the paper stolen from me did not in any way relate to the Gibraltar fortifications."

"Then I'll do my best to get you by the provost guard," Ensign Darrin promised, turning to lead the way back.

"Sir," Dave announced to Lieutenant Abercrombie, commanding the provost guard detachment, "I beg to report, on what I regard as the best of authority, that there is no reason why my countryman, Mr. Cushing, should be detained by you."

"Then that of which he claims to have been

robbed is nothing that could officially interest me?" pressed the British officer.

"I am certain that the matter could not interest a British officer, except in his desire to see a thief caught," Ensign Darrin vouched.

"That is all, then," replied Lieutenant Abercrombie. "Gentlemen, you are at liberty to proceed on your way."

In the meantime the Spanish waiter had slipped back to the theatre.

Dave and Dan saluted, the Englishman doing the same. Then Lieutenant Abercrombie gave each of these brothers in arms a hearty handclasp. The men of the provost guard parted to allow the three Americans to pass on their way.

"And now where do you wish to go, Mr. Cushing?" Dave inquired, after they had passed the British provost guard.

"I suppose you expect me to search for the thief," rejoined the man from the State Department. "But that would now be worse than a waste of time. Gibraltar, quaint Moorish city that it is, is so full of holes in the wall that it would be impossible to find the thief, for he will not venture out again to-night. The best thing I can do will be to go straight to the American admiral, and you gentlemen, I imagine, can take me there."

"A launch will put off from the mole for the

flagship at ten o'clock," Dave informed him.
"We may as well go down to the mole and wait."

Twice, on the way, after leaving the more
crowded parts of the city behind, the three were
challenged by English sentries invisible in the
darkness.

"Who goes there?" came the sentry's hail in
each instance.

"Officers from the American flagship," Darrin
answered for the party.

"Pass on, gentlemen," came the response out
of the darkness.

At all times strict watch over all comers outside the British army service is kept at Gibraltar,
and after dark this vigilance is doubled.

"On a moonless night like this, one would
imagine that Gibraltar, save for the few blocks
of 'city,' held few human beings," murmured
Dan, as the three continued on at a quiet walk
toward the water front. "One gets the impression that there are but a few sentries, sprinkled
here and there, yet we know there are thousands
of British soldiers scattered over this rock."

"Hardly scattered," smiled Dave Darrin. "Except for the guard, men and officers are alike in
barracks, and many of the barracks are at rather
long distances from the fortifications."

Nor are the fortifications to be found along
the water front. Back on the great hill of rock

are gun embrasures, often cut into the face of the rock itself. Back of the embrasures are galleries cut through the stone, and here, in time of siege, the soldiers would stand behind the huge guns.

Gibraltar's harbor is small, though large enough to hold a great fleet. In the days when cannon had shorter range than now, a British fleet might have hidden in the harbor and been secure against all the fleets of the world, for the guns of the huge fortress could have sunk the combined navies of the world, had they attempted to enter the harbor. In these modern days Gibraltar is not so secure, for the heights of Algeciras, in Spain, are only about seven miles away. If Spain were at war with Great Britain, or if any other power took the heights of Algeciras from Spain, guns could be mounted on those heights that would dominate the harbor of Gibraltar. None the less, as long as war exists and the huge stone height of Gibraltar remains, the impression of strong military force will abide with the rock.

Down at the mole a British sentry stopped the trio. Near him stood a corporal and three other soldiers.

"American officers and a friend," replied Ensign Darrin, when halted by this sentry. Then the trio advanced when ordered. Lieutenant Totten, from the 'Hudson,' stepped forward, peered at Darrin and Dalzell, and said to the corporal:

"I recognize these gentlemen as officers of ours."

"And the friend?" inquired the corporal.

"The friend is an American citizen who has business with Admiral Timworth," Dave stated.

"Then it is all right," Lieutenant Totten assured the corporal.

Whereupon the British corporal permitted Cushing to step out on the mole with his companions, Darrin and Dalzell.

"Which is the flagship launch?" asked Darrin.

"The rearmost," answered Lieutenant Totten. "Ours is the only launch here. The two other launches belong to the warships of other powers."

Cushing, while this brief conversation was going on, had walked rapidly along the mole until he reached the farthest launch.

"I want you!" he shouted, bending over suddenly.

He had found and seized by the coat collar the man with the green hat.

Dave and Dan rushed to the spot, hardly knowing what they could do, as they did not want to see the representative of the American State Department lack for backing.

"Pull Cushing away from that fellow," ordered Totten.

"Is that an official order?" Dave flashed back, in a whisper.

"It is," nodded Totten, and faded back into the blackness of the night.

Dave bounded forward. He saw that the launch was one belonging to some liner or merchant ship in the harbor. Three or four men belonging in that launch had leaped to the rescue of Mr. Green Hat. Dave, with one tug, tore Cushing away.

Mr. Green Hat fell back in the launch. Two sailors belonging to that craft cast off the lines at bow and stern, and the launch glided out into the harbor.

"Why didn't you help me, instead of putting the double cross on me?" Cushing demanded, angrily.

"I had my reasons," Ensign Darrin replied, briefly.

"They must have been good ones," muttered Cushing.

"All aboard for the flagship!" announced Lieutenant Totten, in a quiet tone.

"Come along, if you're going out with us," Darrin urged Cushing.

The passengers for the flagship launch were speedily aboard. Other officers were there who had been ashore for the evening.

As the launch was cast off she glided almost

noiselessly across the smooth water of the harbor, followed closely by the shifting rays of a British searchlight on shore. Ever since the great European war had started searchlights stationed on shore had followed the movements of every craft in the harbor at night. Beyond, the flagship's few lights glowed brightly. In a few minutes the party was alongside.

Dave and Dan, after saluting the officer of the deck, and reporting their presence on board, went at once to Dave's quarters.

"There was a good deal of a mix-up, somewhere," Dan announced, at once. "Why should Totten order you to drag Cushing away from Mr. Green Hat, when that rascal had robbed Cushing of valuable government papers?"

"It's too big a puzzle for me," Ensign Darrin admitted, promptly. "But Lieutenant Totten is my superior officer, and the responsibility belongs to him."

For a few minutes the two chums chatted. Dalzell was about to say good night and go to his own quarters, when an orderly rapped at the door, then entered, saluting.

"The admiral's compliments, gentlemen," said the messenger. "The admiral wishes to see Ensigns Darrin and Dalzell at once."

"Our compliments, and we will report at once," Dave answered. Both young officers were now

in uniform, for Dan had left his in Dave's quarters
before going ashore, and the chums had changed
their clothes while chatting. It now remained
only for Dave to reach for his sword and fasten
it on, then draw on white gloves, while Dalzell
went to his quarters, next door, and did the
same.

"What can be in the wind?" whispered Dan.
"This is the first time that Admiral Timworth
has ever expressed any desire to see us. Can it
be that we bungled in some way with the Cushing
business?"

"I'm not going to waste any time in guessing,"
replied Ensign Darrin, as they stepped briskly
along, "when I'm going to have the answer
presented to me so soon."

Then they halted before the entrance to the
admiral's quarters, to learn if it would be agreeable for the admiral to receive them at once.

CHAPTER II

DAN'S THIRTY-THREE-DOLLAR GUESS

A S the two young officers entered the admiral's quarters the curtains were closed behind them by the marine orderly.

Admiral Timworth was seated at his desk. Beside him was Captain Allen, commanding officer of the battleship "Hudson," flagship of the Mediterranean Squadron.

Lieutenant Totten and Cushing were also present.

"Good evening, gentlemen," was Admiral Timworth's greeting, after salutes had been exchanged. "Accidentally, you became spectators, this evening, at a little drama connected with both the diplomatic and the secret service of your country."

The admiral paused, but both young officers remained respectfully at attention, making no response, as none was needed.

"You are aware," continued the admiral, "that Mr. Cushing was knocked down and robbed of an important government paper. Now, it happens that this paper was the key to a code employed by the State and Navy Departments

in communicating with naval commanders
abroad."

This time Dave actually started. The loss of
such a code would be vitally important. The
State and Navy Departments almost invariably
communicate with naval commanders by means
of a secret code, which can be read only by commanders possessing the key. Thus, when cable-
grams are sent from stations in foreign countries,
their import can be understood only by the
officers to whom the communications are addressed.

"That strikes you as a most serious loss, does
it not?" asked Admiral Timworth, smiling.

"Why, yes, sir; so it would seem," Dave answered, bowing.

"The code that was stolen to-night," laughed
the admiral, "will be of but little value to the
government into whose hands it may fall. The
code in question was one that was used in the
year 1880, and has not been employed since.
Nor is it likely ever to be employed again."

Captain Allen joined in the admiral's laugh.

"We had every reason," continued the admiral, "to believe that an attempt would be made
to steal that code ere Mr. Cushing delivered it
to me. In fact, our government allowed it to be
rather widely known that Mr. Cushing had
left Washington to turn over to me a code. So,
of course, Mr. Cushing has been followed. As a

matter of fact, the code that we have been using
for the last six months has not been changed.
I was delighted when I learned that Cushing
had been assaulted and robbed. Mr. Cushing
himself took the loss seriously, for he did not know,
until he came aboard a few moments ago, that
the United States government had hoped he
would be robbed. Lieutenant Totten was sent
ashore, ostensibly to look after the launch, but
in reality, to learn, if possible, whether Cushing's
assailant put off in the launch of another power,
and if so, which power. Ensigns Darrin and
Dalzell, you noted, did you not, the nationality
of the launch in which Mr. Cushing's assailant
escaped?"

"I did not, sir," Dave replied. "It was not
a naval launch, and therefore did not belong to
any ships belonging to the Entente Allies' naval
vessels in port here."

"Then, gentlemen," continued Admiral Timworth, his voice in tones of formal command,
"you will not at any time mention this matter
to any one unless so directed by me. I have
had just one object in sending for you and giving
you this order. For some time our Government
has known that secret efforts are being made
to discredit us with the allied powers of Europe.
I feel rather certain that this fleet, while in the
Mediterranean, will be closely watched by plotters

serving one of the Central European powers, or
else acting on their own account in the hope of
being able to succeed and then claim reward
from that government. Keep your eyes open.
You may meet other spies and have reason to
suspect them to be such. Do not be fooled by
the apparent nationality of any man's name.
A spy uses many names in his course around the
world. Few international spies ever use their
own names. The man in the green hat, who
assaulted Mr. Cushing to-night, is one of the
cleverest of his kind, and perhaps the most able
with whom we shall have to contend. The
fellow's name is supposed to be Emil Gortchky.
At one time or another he has served as spy for
nearly every government in Europe. He is a
daring, dangerous, and wholly unscrupulous fellow. Ensigns Darrin and Dalzell, I sent for you
in order to tell you these things, and to add that
if, during this cruise, you run across the fellow
at any point, you are to report the fact to me
promptly. Of course you will understand that the
seal of official secrecy attaches to all that I have
said. That is all, gentlemen. Good evening."

Saluting, Ensigns Darrin and Dalzell promptly
withdrew. They were still a good deal puzzled.

"I'll come to your quarters in a minute, if
I may," murmured Danny Grin, as he reached
the door of his own cabin.

"I want you to come," Dave answered dryly.

So, in another minute, Dan Dalzell, minus sword and gloves, bobbed into Dave's room.

"Now, what do you make out of all we have heard and seen?" breathed Dalzell tensely.

"Just what the admiral told us," answered Darrin.

"Nothing more?" pressed Dan.

Dave was thoughtful for a few moments before he replied:

"Danny, boy, we have our orders from the commander of the fleet. If we encounter Mr. Green Hat anywhere in the future, we are to report the fact. That is the extent of our instructions, and I think we shall do very well not to think too much about the matter, but to be ready, at all times, to follow our orders."

"I was in hope that you could evolve something more romantic than that," returned Dalzell disappointedly.

"It is very likely," went on Dave judicially, "that we have already had as large a hand in the affair as we are going to have. I doubt if we shall hear anything more of Mr. Green Hat; even if we hear of his further deeds, we are not likely to have any personal part in them."

"I'm disappointed," Dan admitted, rising. "I'm going to bed now, for I have to be up at half-past three, to turn out on watch at eight bells. You, lucky dog, have no watch to stand until after breakfast. Good night, Dave!"

"Good night; and don't dream of Mr. Green Hat," smiled Darrin. "You'll never see him again."

In that prediction Ensign Darrin was destined to find himself fearfully wide of the mark. Mr. Green Hat was not to be so easily dropped from the future calculations of the youngest naval officers on the "Hudson."

None of our readers require any introduction to Dave Darrin and Dan Dalzell, ofttimes known as "Danny Grin." These two fast friends in the naval service were members of "Dick & Co.," a famous sextette of schoolboys in Gridley. Dick Prescott, Greg Holmes, Dave Darrin, Dan Dalzell, Tom Reade and Harry Hazelton first appeared in the pages of "THE GRAMMAR SCHOOL BOYS SERIES," in which volumes were described the early lives of these young American schoolboys.

We found the six boys again in the pages of the "HIGH SCHOOL BOYS SERIES," in the volumes of which the athletic triumphs of Dick & Co. were vividly set forth. In the "HIGH SCHOOL BOYS' VACATION SERIES" were recounted their further adventures.

At the conclusion of their high school careers the six chums separated to seek different fields of endeavor. Dick Prescott and Greg Holmes secured appointments as cadets at the United States Military Academy at West Point, as narrated in the "WEST POINT SERIES." Dave Darrin and Dan Dalzell were nominated as midshipmen to the United States Naval Academy at Annapolis, and all that befell them there is set forth in the "ANNAPOLIS SERIES." The great things that happened to Tom Reade and Harry Hazelton are told in the volumes of the "YOUNG ENGINEERS SERIES." Dick Prescott's and Greg Holmes' adventures in the Army, after graduation from West Point, are set forth in the volumes of the "BOYS OF THE ARMY SERIES."

The "DAVE DARRIN SERIES" is devoted to the lives of Dave Darrin and Dan Dalzell as naval officers, after their graduation from the Naval Academy. We now find them serving as ensigns, this being the lowest rank among commissioned officers of the United States Navy.

The first volume of this series, published under the title, "DAVE DARRIN AT VERA CRUZ," tells the story of Dave's and Dan's initial active service in the United States Navy. That our two young ensigns took an exciting part in the fighting there is known to all our readers.

For some time after the taking of Vera Cruz by the United States forces and the arrival of Regular Army regiments, Dave and Dan continued to serve with constant credit aboard the

"Long Island," stationed at Vera Cruz. Then followed their detachment from the "Long Island," and their return to the United States. They were then ordered to duty with the Mediterranean Squadron, aboard the flagship "Hudson." We already know what befell them on their arrival at their first port of call, the British fortress of Gibraltar, and in the quaint old Moorish city of the same name, which stands between the fortress and the harbor.

Dan soon took his leave of his chum, going to his own quarters for a short sleep before going on duty at eight bells in the morning. Dave, having opportunity to sleep until shortly before breakfast, sat for some minutes pondering over his strange meeting with Mr. Green Hat, whom he now knew as Emil Gortchky, a notorious international spy.

Still puzzling, Darrin turned out the light and dropped into his berth. Once there the habit of the service came strongly upon him. He was between the sheets to sleep, so, with a final sigh, he shut out thoughts of Mr. Green Hat, of the admiral's remarks, and of the whole train of events of the evening. Within a hundred and twenty seconds he was sound asleep. It was an orderly going the rounds in the early morning who spoke to Ensign Darrin and awakened him.

"Is the ship under way?" asked Dave, rolling over and opening his eyes.

"Aye, aye, sir," responded the orderly, who then wheeled and departed.

Dave was quickly out of his berth, and dressed in time to join the gathering throng of the "Hudson's" officers in the ward-room, where every officer, except the captain, takes his meals.

"Have you heard the port for which we're bound, Danny?" Darrin asked his chum.

"Not a word," replied Dalzell, shaking his head.

"Perhaps we shall find out at breakfast," commented Dave.

A minute later the signal came for the officers to seat themselves. Then, after orders had been given to the attentive Filipino boys, who served as mess attendants, a buzz of conversation ran around the table.

Soon the heavy, booming voice of Lieutenant Commander Metson was heard as he asked Commander Dawson, the executive officer:

"Sir, are we privileged to ask our port of destination?"

This is a question often put to the executive officer of a war vessel, for ninety-nine times out of a hunderd he knows the answer. He *may* smile and reply:

"I do not know."

Sometimes the executive officer, who is the captain's confidential man, has good reasons for not divulging the destination of the ship. In that case his denial of knowledge is understood to be only a courteous statement that he does not deem it discreet to name the port of destination.

But in this instance Commander Dawson smiled and replied:

"I will not make any secret of our destination so far as I know it. We are bound for some port on the Riviera. It may be Nice, or perhaps Monte Carlo. I am informed that the admiral has not yet decided definitely. I shall be quite ready to tell you, Mr. Metson, as soon as I know."

"Thank you, sir," courteously acknowledged the lieutenant commander.

During this interval the buzz of conversation had died down. It soon began again.

"The Riviera!" exclaimed Ensign Dalzell jubilantly, though in a low tone intended mainly for his chum's ear. "I have always wanted to see that busy little strip of beach."

The Riviera, as will be seen by reference to a map of Southern Europe, is a narrow strip of land, between the mountains and the sea, running around the Gulf of Genoa. One of the most important watering places on this long strip of beach is Nice, on French soil, where multitudes of health and pleasure seekers flock annually. The mild, nearly tropical climate of this place in winter makes Nice one of the most attractive resorts along the Riviera. Only a few miles distant from Nice is the principality of Monte Carlo, an independent state under a prince who is absolute ruler of his tiny country. Monaco is but two and a quarter miles long, while its width varies from a hundred and sixty-five yards to eleven hundred yards. Yet this "toy country" is large enough to contain three towns of fair size. The most noted town, Monte Carlo, stands mainly on a cliff, and is the location of the most notorious gambling· resort in the world, the "Casino."

"I wonder," suggested one of the younger officers, in a rumbling voice, "if our Government feels that we officers have more money than we need, and so is sending us to a place where we can get rid of it by gambling. What do you say, Darrin?"

"Monte Carlo is one of the noted spots of the world," Dave responded slowly, "and I shall be glad to see a place of which I have heard and read so much. But I shall not gamble at Monte Carlo. I can make better use of my money and of my character."

"Bravo!" agreed Totten.

"How long is that strip of beach, the Riviera?" asked one officer of Lieutenant Commander Wales, the navigating officer.

"From Nice to Genoa, which is what is commonly understood as the real Riviera," replied the navigating officer; "the distance is one hundred and sixteen miles. But, beyond Genoa, on the other side, the beach continues for fifty-six miles to Spezia. On the strip from Genoa to Spezia the shore is so rocky that it has been found necessary to construct eighty-odd tunnels through the headlands for the railway that runs the whole length of the Riviera."

Most of the talk, during that breakfast hour, was about the Riviera, and much of that had to do with Monte Carlo.

"For years I've wanted very particularly to see that town of Monte Carlo," Danny Grin confessed.

"Not to gamble, I hope," replied Dave.

"Millions for sight-seeing, but not a cent for gambling," Dalzell paraphrased lightly.

"Gentlemen," warned Mr. Wales, "don't be too certain that you'll see Monte Carlo on this cruise. Often the weather is too rough for a landing in that vicinity."

"And in that case?" queried Lieutenant Totten.

"In that case," replied Wales, "the usual rule is for the ship to go on to anchorage in the harbor at Genoa."

"Any one know whether the barometer is talking about a storm?" Dalzell asked.

"That's a foolish question," remarked Lieutenant Barnes grouchily.

"Hello!" said Danny Grin, turning half around and eyeing the last speaker. "You here?"

"As usual," nodded Barnes gruffly.

"What was that you said about a foolish question?" demanded Dan.

"I was referring to your habit of asking foolish questions," retorted Barnes.

"Do I ask any more of them than you do?" Dalzell retorted, a bit gruffly.

"You do," Barnes declared, "and that's one of them."

"If I thought I asked more foolish questions than you do, sir," Dan rejoined, laying down his coffee cup, "I'd —"

Here Dalzell paused.

"What would you do?" Barnes insisted.

"On second thought," Dan went on gravely, "I don't believe I'll tell you. It was something desperate that I was thinking of."

"Then drop the idea, Dalzell," scoffed Lieutenant Barnes lightly. "You're hardly the fellow we'd look to for desperate deeds."

"Oh, am I not?" demanded Dan, for once a bit miffed.

Several of the officers glanced up apprehensively.

From necessity, life in the ward-room is an oppressively close one at best. A feud between two officers of the mess is enough to make all hands uncomfortable much of the time.

"Cut it, Barnes," ordered the officer sitting on the right-hand side of Lieutenant Barnes. "Don't start any argument."

"Gentlemen," broke in the paymaster, anxious to change the topic of conversation, "have you gone so far with your meal that a little bad news won't spoil your appetites?"

Most of those present nodded, smilingly.

"Then," continued the paymaster, "I wish to bring up a matter that has been discussed here before. You all know that in some way, owing to the carelessness of some one, there is an unexplained shortage of thirty-three dollars in our mess-fund. You appointed Totten and myself a committee to look into the matter. We now beg to report that the thirty-three dollars cannot be accounted for. What is your pleasure in the matter?"

"I would call it very simple," replied Lieutenant Commander Wales. "Why not levy an assessment upon the members of this mess sufficient to make up the thirty-three dollars? It will amount to very little apiece."

That way of remedying the shortage would have been agreed to promptly, had not Lieutenant Barnes cut in eagerly:

"I've a better plan for making up the shortage. One man can pay it all, as a penalty, and there will be a lot of fun in deciding which member has to pay the penalty."

"What's the idea, Mr. Barnes?" asked the executive officer.

"It's simple enough," Barnes went on, grinning. "Let us set apart the dinner hour on Tuesday evening, say. Every time this mess gets together we hear a lot of foolish questions asked. Now, on Tuesday evening, if any member of this mess asks a question that he can't answer himself, let it be agreed that he pay into the mess a fine of thirty-three dollars to cover the shortage."

"It won't work," objected Totten. "Every officer at this table will be on his guard not to ask any questions at all."

"In that case," proposed Barnes, "let the rule hold over on each successive Tuesday evening until the victim is found and has paid his fine."

"It sounds like sport," agreed Dave Darrin.

"It will be sport to see the victim 'stung' and made to pay up," grinned Dan Dalzell.

"And I think I know, already," contended Lieutenant Barnes, "which officer will pay that shortage."

"Are you looking at me with any particular significance?" demanded Danny Grin.

"I am," Barnes admitted.

"Oh, well, then, we shall see what we shall see," quoth Dalzell, his color rising.

The scheme for fixing the thirty-three-dollar penalty was quickly agreed upon. In fact, the plan had in it many of the exciting elements of a challenge.

Darrin left the mess to go on duty. Dan found him presently.

"Say," murmured Danny Grin, in an aside, "do you think Barnes will be very angry when he pays over that thirty-three dollars?"

"I haven't yet heard that he is to pay it," Dave answered quietly.

"But he *is*," Dalzell asserted.

"How's that?"

"I'm going to make it my business," Dan went on, "to see that Barnes is the victim of the very scheme that he proposed. He will ask a question that he can't answer, and he'll do it when Tuesday evening comes around."

"Don't be too sure of that," Dave warned him. "Barnes may not be exactly the most amiable officer aboard, but at least he's a very keen chap. If you are forming any plans for making Barnes pay, look out, Dan, that your scheme doesn't recoil upon yourself!"

"Wait and see," Dalzell insisted. "I tell you, Barnes is going to pay that thirty-three dollars into the mess treasury!"

CHAPTER III

THE STARTLER AT MONTE CARLO

THE frowning crags of Monaco confronted the United States battleship "Hudson."

Here and there the rocky eminences were broken by tiny strips of white beach. In comparison with the crags the great, floating fighting machine looked like a pigmy, indeed.

It was toward evening, and the day was Tuesday. Darrin and Dalzell, both off duty for the time being, strolled along the battleship's quarterdeck, gazing shoreward.

"It's almost too bad that the times are so civilized," murmured Danny Grin. "That little toy principality would make an ideal pirates' nest."

"I fancy Monaco has done duty enough in that line in the past centuries," smiled Darrin. "I have been reading up a bit on the history of Monaco. Piracy flourished here as late as the fourteenth century. Even rather late in the eighteenth century every ship passing close to this port had to pay toll. And to-day, through its vast gambling establishments, visited by thousands every week, Monaco reaches out **and** still takes its toll from all the world."

"It won't take any from me," smiled Dalzell.

"That is because you're a disciplined human being, and you've too much character and honesty to gamble," Darrin went on. "But think, with a pitying sigh, of the thousands of poor wretches who journey to Monaco, enter the Casino at Monte Carlo, part with their money and their honor, and then pass into one of the gardens, there to blow their brains out.

"We shall get a glimpse of the place to-night," Dave continued. "I will admit that I have a good deal of curiosity to see it. So I am glad that we have shore leave effective after dinner. Still, we shan't see anything like the crowd or the picture that we might see if Europe were at peace."

"This is Tuesday night," Dan warned his chum.

"Yes; the night to avoid dangerous questions at mess," Dave smiled. "Dan, are you still going to try to catch Barnes?"

"Watch me," winked Dalzell.

"Look out, Dan! Such a trap may be set at both ends."

But Dalzell winked once more, then allowed his mouth to expand in that contortion which had won him the nick name of "Danny Grin."

Dave soon forgot Dalzell's threat of trouble for the evening. It had passed out of his mind by the time that Ensign Darrin entered the wardroom. Yet soon after the officers had seated themselves the executive officer announced:

"In the interest of fair play to all I deem it best to warn you, gentlemen, that to-night is the night when the first gentleman who asks a question that he cannot himself answer is liable to a penalty of thirty-three dollars to make up the deficit in the mess treasury."

There were nods and grins, and shakings of heads. Not an officer present had any idea that *he* could be caught and made to pay the penalty.

As the meal progressed Lieutenant Commander Wales finally turned to one of the Filipino waiters and inquired:

"Is there any of the rare roast beef left?"

"Don't you know yourself, Wales?" demanded Totten quickly.

"Why, er — no-o," admitted Mr. Wales, looking much puzzled. "Why should I?"

"Then haven't you asked a question that you can't answer?" demanded Totten mischievously.

"That's hardly a fair catch, is it?" demanded the navigating officer, looking annoyed.

"It is not a fair catch," broke in the executive officer incisively. "Any gentleman here has a perfect right to ask the waiter questions about the food supply without taking chances of being subjected to a penalty."

"I bow to the decision, sir," replied Lieutenant Totten. "I merely wished to have the question settled."

Some of those present breathed more easily; others yet dreaded to become victims of a penalty proposition that many now regretted having voted for.

As the dessert came on Dan Dalzell turned to Dave.

"Darrin," he said, "can you tell me why it is that a woodchuck never leaves any dirt heaped up around the edge of his hole?"

Dave reflected, looking puzzled for a moment. Then he shook his head as he answered:

"Dalzell, I'm afraid I don't know why."

"Of course *you* know why, Dalzell," broke in Lieutenant Barnes warningly.

"Perhaps I do know," Dan replied, nodding his head slowly. "However, perhaps some other gentleman would like the chance of answering the question."

Instantly a dozen at least of the officers became interested in answering the question. To each reply or guess, however, Dalzell shook his head.

"If everyone who wants it has had a try at the answer," suggested the executive officer, "then we will call upon Mr. Dalzell to inform us why a woodchuck, in digging his hole, leaves no dirt piled up around the entrance."

There was silence while Dan replied easily:

"It's perfectly simple. Instead of beginning at the surface of the ground and digging downward, the woodchuck begins at the bottom of the hole and digs up toward the light and air."

As Dalzell offered this explanation he faced Lieutenant Barnes, who was eying him scoffingly.

When Dan had finished his explanation there was a puzzled silence for an instant. But Dan's half-leer irritated Lieutenant Barnes. Then came the explosion.

"Shaw!" snorted Barnes. "That's an explanation that doesn't explain anything. It's a fool answer. How does the woodchuck, if he digs up from the bottom of the hole, ever manage to get to the bottom of the hole to make his start there?"

"Oh, well," answered Dan slowly, "that's your question, Mr. Barnes."

"My question?" retorted the lieutenant. "What do you mean?"

"If I understand aright," Dan went on, "you asked how the woodchuck manages to get to the bottom of the hole before he begins to dig."

"That's right," nodded the lieutenant, stiffly.

"That's just the idea," Dan grinned. "I am calling upon you to answer the question that you just asked. You must tell us how the woodchuck manages to get to the bottom of the hole in order to start digging upward."

It required perhaps two seconds for the joke to dawn on the other officers at the long mess table. Then an explosion of laughter sounded, and every eye was turned toward Lieutenant Barnes.

"That isn't fair!" roared the lieutenant, leaping to his feet. "That was a trap! It wasn't a fair catch."

Barnes's face was very red. His voice quivered with indignation.

But Dan Dalzell was smiling coolly as he retorted:

"I'll leave it to the mess if Barnes hasn't asked a question that he can't answer."

"You're caught, Barnes!" roared half a dozen voices, and more laughter followed.

"You asked a question, Barnes, and you can't answer it," came from others.

"That thirty-three dollars will come in handy," called another.

"Pay up like a man, Barnes."

"That's right. Pay up! You're caught."

The lieutenant's face grew redder, but he sat down and tried to control his wrath.

"It doesn't seem like a fairly incurred penalty," declared Barnes, as soon as he could make himself heard, "but of course I'll abide by the decision of the mess."

"Then I move," suggested Wales, "that we leave the question to a committee of three to decide whether Mr. Barnes has been properly caught in the fine that he himself was the one to propose. For committee I would suggest the executive officer, the paymaster and the chaplain."

Informally that suggestion was quickly adopted. The three officers named withdrew to a corner of the ward-room, where they conversed in low tones, after which they returned to their seats.

"Gentlemen," announced the executive officer, "the committee has discussed the problem submitted to it, and the members of the committee are unanimously agreed that Mr. Barnes fairly and fully incurred the penalty that he himself suggested the other morning."

Barnes snorted, but was quick to recover sufficiently to bow in the direction of the executive officer.

"Then I accept the decision, sir," announced the lieutenant huskily. "At the close of the meal I will pay thirty-three dollars into the mess treasury."

Barnes tried to look comfortable, but he refused to glance in the direction of Danny Grin.

"Did I catch him?" whispered Dalzell to his chum.

"You did," Dave agreed quickly. "Barnes

must feel pretty sore over the way his plan turned out."

There was much laughter during the rest of the meal, and Barnes had to stand for much chaffing, which he bore with a somewhat sullen look. As the officers rose none offered to leave the ward-room. All stood by waiting to see Barnes hand thirty-three dollars to the paymaster.

"Here is the money," announced Barnes, handing a little wad of bills to the paymaster.

"Count it, Pay!" piped a voice from the rear of the crowd, but it was not Dan who spoke.

Lieutenant Barnes had the grace to leave the ward-room without stamping, but in the nearest passageway he encountered Ensigns Darrin and Dalzell.

"I suppose you are chuckling over the way I dropped right into your trap," snapped Barnes to Dan. "But do you call it a fair kind of trap?"

"What was the committee's decision on the subject?" inquired Dan, softly.

"Oh, I'll admit that the decision went against me," answered the lieutenant, scowling. "How will you like it if I promise to pay you back fully for that trick? Are you willing that I should?"

"If your mind is set on paying me back," Danny Grin responded, "then my willingness would have very little to do with your conduct. But I am willing to make you a promise, sir."

"What is that?" asked the lieutenant, quite testily.

"If you attempt to pay me back, sir, and succeed, I'll agree to take my medicine with an appearance of greater good humor than you displayed a few minutes ago."

"Huh!" sniffed Mr. Barnes.

"Danny boy," broke in Dave, "I don't want to spoil a pleasant conversation, but I would like to remind you that, if we are to make much of our evening ashore, we shall do well to change to 'cits' at once. The launch leaves the side in fifteen minutes."

"You'll excuse me, won't you, sir?" begged Dalzell, favoring the lieutenant with an extremely pleasant smile.

The chums went to their respective cabins, where they quickly made the change from uniform to citizen's dress, commonly called "cits."

Promptly the launch left the "Hudson's" side, but both young ensigns were aboard. At least a dozen other officers and a score of seamen were also aboard the launch, which was to return for forty more seamen who held the coveted shore leave.

Yet the reader is not to suppose that either officers or men were going ashore with any notion of gambling. An American naval officer, with his status of "officer and gentleman," would risk a severe rebuke from his commanding officer if he were to seat himself to play in any gambling resort. As for the enlisted men, the "jackies," they are not of the same piece of cloth as the jovial, carousing seamen of the old-time Navy. The "jackies" of to-day are nearly all extremely youthful; they are clean-cut, able, ambitious young fellows, much more inclined to study than to waste their time in improper resorts.

So, while most of the officers and men now going ashore were likely to drop in at the Casino, for the sake of seeing the sights there, it was not in the least to be feared that any would engage in the gambling games.

When the launch landed in the little harbor, drivers of automobiles and carriages clamored for fares.

"Are we going to ride up to the Casino?" Dan asked his chum.

"If you'd rather," Dave assented. "But, unless you feel tired, let us stroll along and see every bit of the way."

"These natives are all jabbering French," complained Dalzell, as the chums set out to walk over the steep, well-worn roads, "but it isn't the kind of French we were taught at Annapolis."

"Can't you understand them?" asked Dave.

"Hardly a word."

"If you have to talk with any of the natives," Dave advised, "speak your French slowly, and ask the person you're addressing to do the same."

Though the way was steep, it was not a long road. Dave and Dan soon reached the upper, rocky plain, edged by cliffs, on which the Casino and some of the hotels and other buildings stand.

"If it weren't for the gambling," murmured Dan to his friend, "I'd call this a beautiful enough spot to live and die in."

"As it is, a good many men and women manage to die here," Darrin returned gravely.

The Casino was surrounded by beautiful gardens, in which were many rare tropical trees and shrubs. From the Casino came the sound of orchestral music. Throngs moved about on the verandas; couples or little groups strolled through the gardens. Inside, the play had hardly begun. Gambling does not reach its frantic height until midnight.

"We shall feel out of place," mused Dave aloud. "Dan, we really should have known better than to come here in anything but evening dress. You see that every one else is in full regalia."

"Perhaps we'd better keep on the edge of the crowd," responded Danny Grin. "There is enough to be seen here, for one evening, without entering the Casino."

Though Dave intended to enter the Casino later, he decided, for the present, to take in the full beauty of the night in the gardens. There were electric lights everywhere, which outshone the brilliance of the moon.

"Hello!" whispered Dan, suddenly. "There's an old friend of ours."

"Who?"

"Mr. Green Hat," Dan whispered impressively.

Instantly Dave Darrin became intensely interested, though he had no intimation of what this second meeting portended. That Mr. Green Hat was destined to play a highly tragic rôle in his life, Darrin, of course, had no inkling at that moment.

"There he is!" whispered Dalzell, pointing, as the chums stood screened by a flowering bush.

"We'll watch that rascal!" Dave proposed promptly. "I wonder if he has followed the 'Hudson' here with a view to attempting more mischief against our Government. Whatever his game is, I am going to take a peep at the inside of it if a chance comes my way!"

CHAPTER IV

MR. GREEN HAT'S NEW RÔLE

MR. GREEN HAT, on this occasion, had discarded the article of headwear that had given him that nickname with the young ensigns.

Instead, Gortchky wore an opera hat, with evening dress of the most fashionable description. On his broad white expanse of vest there glittered a foreign decoration.

Though he walked alone, and affected an air of indifference to his surroundings, Darrin was of the impression that the spy was looking alertly for some one.

"Of course it may happen," said Dave to his friend, "that the fellow is foolish enough to come here for the purpose of throwing away at the gaming tables the money he earns by his questionable services to some plotting international ring. Yet that seems hardly likely, either, for Gortchky must be a man of tremendous energy, to render the thrilling services that are demanded of a spy or an international trouble-maker."

Now the two chums left the place where they

had been standing behind the bush, to stroll along slowly, all the while keeping Gortchky in sight.

Dave nudged his chum as, at a turn in the path, the spy came face to face with a woman clad in a beautiful evening gown.

Raising his hat, and making a courteous bow to the woman, who returned the greeting, Gortchky exchanged half a dozen sentences with her. Then the pair separated, though not before Dave and Dan had obtained, under the electric light, a good view of the young woman's face. Her dark beauty, her height and grace, gave her a queenly air.

Stepping into another path, Dave and Dan were soon on the trail of Gortchky once more, without having been obliged to pass the young woman face to face.

"I wonder if she's a 'spy-ess'?" murmured Dan.

"It is just as well to be suspicious of any one whom Gortchky appears to know well," Dave answered, slowly, in a low voice.

"I beg pardon, sir," broke in a sailor from the "Hudson," stepping forward and saluting the officers. "May I speak with you, sir?"

It was Dan to whom he spoke, and it was Dan who answered:

"Certainly, Martin."

"The spy came face to face with a woman."

Martin was one of the gun-pointers in Dalzell's division.

"Linton, one of our men, has been hurt, and rather badly, by falling off a boulder that he climbed not far from here, sir. I thought I would ask the ensign what to do with Linton."

"How badly is he hurt?" asked Ensign Dalzell.

"I think his right leg is broken, sir. Colby is with him, and I came in search of you, sir, as I was certain I saw you here."

"Is Linton far from here?" asked Dalzell.

"Less than a quarter of a mile, sir."

"Lead the way, Martin, and I'll follow you. Dave, you'll excuse me for a little while, won't you?"

"Certainly," nodded Ensign Darrin. Dave wished to remain where he was, in order to keep an eye over Gortchky's movements, and Dan knew it. So the chums parted for the present.

"Now, I'll see if I can pick up Gortchky again," reflected Ensign Darrin. "He appears to have given me the slip."

Dave went ahead, more briskly than he had been moving before, in the hope of sighting the spy.

Out of the Casino had staggered a young man, despair written on his face, hopelessness in his very air. Plunging into the garden this stranger made his way hastily through it, keeping on until he came to the field where pigeon shoots are held from time to time.

Dave, at the edge of the garden, saw the young man step past the shrubbery and go on into the darkness beyond. Under the last rays of light Ensign Darrin saw something glitter in the stranger's hand.

"That fellow has just drawn a revolver!" flashed through Darrin's mind. "Now, what mischief can he be up to?"

Led onward by some fascination that he did not understand, the young naval officer followed.

In his excitement and desperation the man did not notice that he was being followed.

Halting under the heavy foliage of a tree, the stranger glanced down at the weapon in his hand and shuddered. This foolish young man, haunting the gambling tables until he had ruined himself, and seeing nothing now ahead of him in life, was bent upon self-destruction.

Sometimes there are several such suicides at Monte Carlo in a single week. If unprovided with other means for ending his life, the suicide sometimes hurls himself over the edge of one of the steep cliffs.

Suicides, of course, have a depressing effect on other players, so those in authority at the Casino take every means of hushing up these tragedies as effectively as possible.

"There is really nothing left in life," muttered the young man huskily, as he stared at the weapon in his hand. He spoke in French, but Darrin heard and understood him.

Then the desperate one raised the weapon, pointing the muzzle at his head.

At that instant there was a quick step out of the darkness, and Dave reached the stranger. The latter, startled, drew back, but not in time to prevent Darrin's grip of steel from resting on his right wrist.

Wrench! Dave had the pistol in his own hands, at the same time murmuring:

"You will pardon me, I trust."

Ensign Darrin broke the weapon open at the breach. From the chamber he removed the cartridges, dropping them into his pocket. With another swift movement Dave flung the pistol so far that it dropped over the edge of a cliff.

"You will pardon me, I trust, sir, for throwing your property away in that fashion," Dave apologized, in the best French he could summon.

"Since it is the very last item of my property that was left to me, perhaps it can matter but little that I am deprived of it," said the stranger, smiling wanly. "The cliff is still left to me, however. I can easily follow the pistol."

"But you are not going to jump over the cliff," Darrin assured him energetically.

"And why are you so certain of that?" demanded the stranger.

Dave looked keenly at his companion before he replied:

"Because, sir, your face is that of a man — not of a coward. Suicide is the act of a coward. It is the resort of one who frankly admits that his troubles are greater than he has the manhood to bear. Now, you have, when one regards you closely, the look of a man and a gentleman."

"Thank you for your good opinion, sir," replied the stranger, bowing. "I will say that I was born a gentleman."

"And you still are one, and a man, as well as a gentleman," Dave continued, gently. "Therefore, you are not afraid to face life."

"What is there left to me to make life worth living?" queried the stranger.

"Why should you have the least desire to die?" Dave countered.

"I have lost all my money."

"That is a very slight matter," Darrin argued. "Lost all your money, have you? Why, my dear fellow, there's a lot more in the world."

"But none of the money now in the world is mine," urged the desperate one.

"Then make a part of the world's money yours," the young naval officer retorted, smilingly.

"I have never worked," replied the stranger stiffly.

"Why not?" Dave pressed.

"I never had need to."

"But now you have the need, and working for money will bring some novelty into your life," the young ensign insisted.

"Did I not tell you that I was born a gentleman?" inquired the young man, raising his eyebrows. "A gentleman never works!"

"Some gentlemen don't," Dave admitted. "But they are the wrong kind of gentlemen."

"If I mistake not," quizzed the stranger keenly, "you are a gentleman, yourself."

"I trust that I am," Dave responded gravely.

"Then do you work?"

"More hours a day than any laborer does," Darrin answered promptly. "I am a naval officer."

"Ah, but that is a career of honor — of glory!" cried the stranger.

"And so is any honest job of work that a man takes up in earnest and carries through to the best of his ability," Dave Darrin returned with warmth.

"But you see, sir," argued the stranger, though now he was smiling, "you have been trained to a profession. I never was so trained."

"You are young?"

"Twenty-four."

"Then you are young enough to change your

mind and recognize the dignity of labor," Darrin continued. "You are also young enough and, unless I mistake you, bright enough to win a very good place in life for yourself. And you are man enough, now you have had time to think it over, to see the wickedness of destroying yourself. Man, *make* yourself instead."

"I'll do it! I will make myself!" promised the stranger, with a new outburst of emotion.

"And you will never again allow yourself to become so downcast that you will seek to destroy yourself?"

"Never!"

"I am satisfied," Dave said gravely. "You are a man of honor, and therefore are incapable of breaking your word. Your hand!"

Their hands met in ardent clasp. Then Darrin took out his card case, tendering his card to the stranger.

Instantly the young man produced his own card case, and extended a bit of pasteboard, murmuring:

"I am M. le Comte de Surigny, of Lyons, France."

It was too dark to read the cards there, but Dave gave his own name, and again the young men shook hands.

"But I am forgetting my comrade," Dave cried suddenly. "He was to return in a few minutes, and will not know where to find me."

"And I have detained you, with my own wretched affairs!" cried the young count reproachfully. "I must not trespass upon your time another second."

"Why not walk along with me and meet my friend?" Dave suggested.

"With pleasure."

Dave and the young French count stepped along briskly until they came to the spot where Dalzell had left his chum. Two or three minutes later Dan hove into sight.

Dan and the Count of Surigny were introduced, and some chat followed. Then the Count frankly told of the service that Darrin had just rendered him.

"That is Dave!" glowed Dan. "He's always around in time to be of use to some one."

In the distance a shot rang out — only one. The Count of Surigny shuddered.

"You understand, do you not?" he asked.

"I am afraid so," Dave sadly responded.

As they stood there four men with a litter hurried past toward the place whence the sound of the shot had come.

"The police of Monte Carlo," murmured the Count of Surigny.

Presently, at a distance, the three onlookers beheld the four men and the litter moving stealthily along, but not toward the Casino. The litter was occupied by a still form over which a cover had been thrown.

"You have shown me the way of true courage!" murmured the Count of Surigny, laying an affectionate hand on Ensign Darrin's shoulder.

The chums and their new acquaintance strolled along for a few moments. Then the Count suddenly exclaimed:

"But I am intruding, and must leave you."

"You surely are not intruding," Dave told him. "We are delighted with your company."

"Wholly so," Dan added.

But the Count felt himself to be an interloper, and so insisted on shaking hands again and taking his departure.

"I shall see or write you presently," said the Count. He had already obtained the fleet address, and knew, in addition, that he could write at any time through the Navy Department at Washington.

"Will he make good?" asked Danny Grin wistfully, as he peered after the departing form.

"It's an even chance," Dave replied. "Either that young man will go steadily up, or else he will go rapidly down. It is sometimes a terrible thing to be born a gentleman — in the European sense. Few of the Count's friends will appreciate him if he starts in upon a career of effort. But, even though he goes down, he will struggle bravely at the outset. Of that I feel certain."

"I wonder what has become of Gortchky?" remarked Ensign Dalzell.

That industrious spy, however, was no longer the pursued; he had become the pursuer.

From a little distance Gortchky had espied Dave and the Count chatting, and had witnessed the introduction to Dalzell. A man of Mr. Green Hat's experience with the world did not need many glances to assure himself that the Count had lost his last franc at the gambling table.

Gortchky was not at Monte Carlo without abundant assistance. So, as the Count, head down, and reflecting hard, strolled along one of the paths, a man bumped into him violently.

"Ten thousand pardons, Monsieur!" cried the bumper, in a tone of great embarrassment. "It was stupid of me. I —"

"Have no uneasiness, my friend," smiled the Count. "It was I who was stupid. I should have looked where I was going."

Courteous bows were exchanged, and the two separated. But the man who had bumped into the Count now carried inside his sleeve the Count's empty wallet, which was adorned with the crest of Surigny.

This wallet was promptly delivered to another.

Five minutes later, as the Count strolled along, Emil Gortchky called out behind him:

"Monsieur! Pardon me, but I think you must have dropped your wallet."

"If I have, the loss is trifling indeed," smiled the Count, turning.

Gortchky held out the wallet, then struck a match. By the flame the Count beheld his own crest.

"Yes, it is mine," replied the Count, "and I thank you for your kindness."

"Will Monsieur do me the kindness, before I leave him, to make sure that the contents of the wallet are intact?" urged Gortchky.

"It will take but an instant," laughed the Count of Surigny. "See! I will show you that the contents are intact!"

As he spoke he opened the wallet. A packet of paper dropped to the ground. In astonishment the Count bent over to pick up the packet. M. Gortchky struck another match.

"Let us go nearer to an electric light, that you may count your money at your ease, Monsieur," suggested Gortchky.

Like one in a daze the Count moved along with Gortchky. When sufficiently in the light, Surigny, with an expression of astonishment, found that he was the possessor of thirty twenty-franc notes.

"I did not know that I had this!" cried the Count. "How did I come to overlook it?"

"It is but a trifle to a man of your fortune," cried M. Gortchky gayly.

"It is all I have in the world!" sighed the young man. "And I am still amazed that I possess so much."

"Poor?" asked Gortchky, in a voice vibrating with sympathy. "And you so young, and a gentleman of old family! Monsieur, it may be that this is a happy meeting. Perhaps I may be able to offer you the employment that befits a gentleman."

Then Gortchky lowered his voice, almost whispering:

"For I am in the diplomatic service, and have need of just such an attaché as you would make. Young, a gentleman, and of charming manners! Your intellect, too, I am sure, is one that would fit you for eminence in the diplomatic service."

"The mere mention of the diplomatic service attracts me," confessed M. le Comte wistfully.

"Then you shall have your fling at it!" promised M. Gortchky. "But enough of this. You shall talk it over with me to-morrow. Diplomacy, you know, is all gamble, and the gambler makes the best diplomat in the world. For to-night, Monsieur, you shall enjoy yourself! If I know anything of gaming fate, then you are due to reap a harvest of thousands with your few francs to-night. I can see it in your face that your luck is about to turn. An evening of calm, quiet play, Monsieur, and in the morning you and I will arrange for your entrance into the diplomatic world. *Faites votre jeux!* (Make your wagers.) Wealth to-night, and a career to-morrow! Come! To the Casino!"

CHAPTER V

DANNY GRIN FIGHTS A SMILE

SIDE by side Dave and Dan strolled through the vast main salon of the Casino.

Here at tables were groups of men and women. Each player hoped to quit the tables that night richer by thousands. Most of them were doomed to leave poorer, as chance is always in favor of the gambling institution and always against the player.

"It's a mad scene," murmured Dan, in a low voice.

"You are looking on now at an exhibition of what is probably the worst, and therefore the most dangerous, human vice," Dave replied. "Bad as drunkenness is, gambling is worse."

"What is at the bottom of the gambling mania?" Dan asked thoughtfully.

"Greed," Dave responded promptly. "The desire to possess property, and to acquire it without working for it."

"Some of these poor men and women look as if they were working hard indeed," muttered Dan, in almost a tone of sympathy.

"They are not working so much as suffering," Dave rejoined. "Study their faces, Danny boy. Can't you see greed sticking out all over these countenances? Look at the hectic flush in most of the faces. And — look at that man!"

A short, stout man sprang up from a table, his face ghastly pale and distorted as though with terror. His eyes were wild and staring. He chattered incoherently as he hastened away with tottering steps. Then his hands gripped his hair, as though about to tear it from his head.

A few of the players in this international congress of greed glanced at the unfortunate man, who probably had just beggared himself, shrugged their shoulders, and turned their fascinated eyes back to the gambling table.

One woman, young and charming, reached up to her throat, unfastening and tossing on the table a costly diamond necklace and pendant.

"Now," she laughed hysterically, "I may go on playing for another hour."

The Casino's representative in charge at that table smiled and shook his head.

"We accept only money, madame," he said, with a grave bow.

"But I have no more money — with me," flashed back the young woman, her cheeks burning feverishly.

"I regret, madame," insisted the Casino's

man. Then an attendant, at a barely perceptible
sign from the *croupier*, as the man in charge of
the table is called, stepped up behind the young
woman, bent over her and murmured:

"If you care to leave the table for a few minutes,
madame; there are those close at hand who will
advance you money on your necklace."

The young woman pouted at first. In another
instant there was a suppressed shout at the table.
A player had just won four thousand francs.

"I must have money!" cried the young woman,
springing from her chair. "This is destined to
be my lucky night, and I must have money!"

As though he had been waiting for his prey,
the attendant was quickly by the woman's side.
Bowing, he offered his arm. The man, attendant
though he was, was garbed in evening dress.
Without a blush the woman moved away on this
attendant's arm.

"Shall we move on?" asked Dan.

"Not just yet," urged Darrin, in an undertone. "I am interested in the further fate of
that foolish young woman."

Within five minutes she had returned. Her
former seat had been reserved for her; the young
woman dropped into it.

"You have enough money now?" asked the
woman at her left.

"I have money," pouted the pretty young

woman, "but be warned by me. The pawnbrokers at Monte Carlo are robbers. The fellow would advance me only six thousand francs, whereas my husband paid a hundred thousand for that necklace."

A moment later the young woman was absorbed in the wild frenzy of play.

"And that attendant undoubtedly gets a handsome commission from the pawnbroker," murmured Darrin in his chum's ear. "Greed here is in the very air; none can escape it who lingers."

"How much have you lost, Darrin?" called a bantering voice in Dave's ear.

The speaker was Lieutenant Totten.

"About as much, I imagine, as you have, sir," was Darrin's smiling answer.

"Meaning that you now have as much money as when you entered the place?" answered the lieutenant, banteringly.

"Exactly," returned Darrin. "I have only to study the faces here to know better than to risk even a franc-piece at one of these tables."

"And you, Dalzell?" inquired Totten.

"I haven't any French money, anyway," grinned Dan.

"Not at all necessary to have French money," laughed Totten. "Any kind of real money is good here — as long as it lasts. Every nation on earth is represented here to-night, and the attendants know the current exchange rate for any kind of good money that is coined or printed. Look closely about you and you will see other things that are worth nothing. There are men here, some of them limping, others showing the pallor of illness, who are undoubtedly French, English or Italian officers, injured at the front and sent home to hospitals. Being still unfitted to return to their soldier duties at the front, they are passing time here and indulging in their mania for gambling. And here, too, you will see wealthy French, Italian, English or Russian civilians who have returned to Monte Carlo to gamble, though later on they are pretty certain to be held up to contempt at home for gambling money away·here instead of buying government war bonds at home."

"You have been here before?" Dave asked.

"Oh, yes," nodded Totten, "and as I do not play, and would not do so in any circumstances, this place has not much interest for me."

"I can hardly imagine," said Ensign Darrin, gravely, "that I shall ever bother to pay a second visit here."

"It's a good deal of a bore," yawned Lieutenant Totten, behind his hand. "I am glad to note that most of the people here look like Europeans. I should hate to believe that many Americans could be foolish enough to come here."

At that moment a stout, red-faced man rose from a table near by, his voice booming as he laughed:

"I have lost only sixteen thousand francs. I shall be sure to come back and have my revenge. In Chicago my signature is good at any time for a million dollars — for five million francs!"

Many eyes followed this speaker wistfully. With such wealth as his how many months of frenzied pleasure they might have at Monte Carlo!

"One American idiot, at least," muttered Totten, in disgust. "Or else he's a liar or braggart.'

Madly the play went on, the faces of the players growing more flushed as the hour grew later.

Totten moved along with a bored air.

"I guess he's going," said Dan. "I don't blame him for being tired of the place. It's like a human menagerie."

"We'll go, then," agreed Dave. "Surely I have seen enough of the Casino. I shall never care to revisit it."

"Ah, here you are, my dear fellows!" exclaimed a musical voice. "And the Countess Ripoli has asked me to present you to her. She is eager to know if you American officers are as wonderful as I have told her."

The speaker was Dandelli, a handsome, boyish-looking, ɪrank-faced young Italian naval officer with whom Darrin and Dalzell had become acquainted at Gibraltar.

The Countess Ripoli, to whom Dandelli now presented the two young ensigns, was a woman in the full flower of her beauty at twenty-five or so. Tall, willowy, with a perfect air, her wonderful eyes, in which there was a touch of Moorish fire, were calculated to set a young man's heart to beating responses to her mood. Attired in the latest mode of Paris, and wearing only enough jewels to enhance her great beauty, the Countess chose to be most gracious to the young ensigns. Dave thought her a charming young woman; Dan Dalzell nearly lost his head.

From a distance Emil Gortchky looked on, a quiet smile gleaming in his eyes.

"Dandelli is a fool, who will do any pretty woman's bidding," mused the spy. "Madame Ripoli can play with him. Also I believe she will surely ensnare for me at least one of the Americans. Which, I wonder? But then why should I care which? The Ripoli knows how to manage such affairs far better than I do."

For the Countess was another of the many dangerous tools with which Mr. Green Hat plied his wicked trade.

If the Countess, as unscrupulous as Gortchky himself, could ensnare either of these young officers with her fascinations, he was likely to be that much the weaker, and a readier prey for the trap that Emil Gortchky was arranging.

"Dandelli," murmured the Countess sweetly, in French, "you will wish, I know, to talk with your dear friend, Mr. Darrin, so I must look to Mr. Dalzell to offer me his arm."

Dan was ready, with a bow, to offer the Countess Ripoli his arm, and to escort her in the direction which she indicated.

It was to one of the verandas that the Countess led the way. As she chatted she laughed and looked up at Dan with her most engaging expression. There were other promenaders on the veranda, though not many, for the furious fascination of gambling tables kept nearly all the frequenters of the place inside.

"You have played to-night?" asked the Countess, again glancing sweetly up into the young naval officer's face.

"Not to-night," Dan replied.

"But you will doubtless play later?" she insisted.

"I haven't gambled to-night, nor shall I gamble on any other night," Dan replied pleasantly.

"But why?" demanded the Countess, looking puzzled.

"Gambling does not fit in with my idea of honesty," replied Dalzell quite bluntly.

CHAPTER VI

DAVE RUNS INTO A REAL THRILL

I DO not understand," murmured the Countess.

"I know that the European idea of gambling is very different from that entertained by most people in my country," Dan went on pleasantly. "To the greater number of Americans, gambling is a method of getting other people's money away from them without working for it."

"And that is why you term it dishonest?" asked the Countess.

"Yes," replied Dan frankly. "And, in addition, it is a wicked waste of time that could be put to so many good uses."

Countess Ripoli shrugged her fine shoulders, and looked up once more at the young officer. But Dan was smiling back coolly at her.

"You have not a flattering idea of the Europeans?" she asked.

"Quite to the contrary," Dan assured her.

"Yet you think we are both weak and dishonest, because we use our time to poor advantage and because so many of us find Monte Carlo, delightful?" she pressed him.

"Not all Europeans frequent Monte Carlo,"
Dalzell answered.

"May I ask my new American friend why *he*
should waste his time here?" laughed the Countess.

"I do not believe I have exactly wasted my
time," Dan replied. "A naval officer, or any
other American, may well spend some of his
time here in gaining a better knowledge of human
nature. Surely, there is much of human
nature to be seen here, even though it be not one
of the better sides."

"What is the bad trait, or the vice, that one be-
holds most at Monte Carlo?" the Countess asked.

"Greed," Dan rejoined promptly.

"And dishonesty?"

"Much of that vice, no doubt," Dan continued.
"To-night there must be many a man here who
is throwing away money that his family needs,
yet he will never tell his wife that he lost his
money over a table at Monte Carlo. Again,
there must be many a woman here throwing
away money in large sums, and she, very likely,
will never tell her husband the truth. Let us
say that, in both sexes, there are a hundred
persons here to-night who will be dishonest
toward their life partners afterward. And then,
perhaps, many a young bachelor, who, betrothed
to some good woman, is learning his first lessons
in greed and deceit. And some young girls, too,

who are perhaps learning the wrong lessons in
life. I know of one very young man here who
tried to blow out his brains to-night. For the
sake of a few hours, or perhaps a few weeks,
over the gaming tables of Monte Carlo, he had
thrown away everything that made life worth
living. Any man who gambles bids good-by to
the finer things of life."

Dan's slow, halting French made the Countess
listen very attentively, that she might understand just what he said. She puckered her brow
thoughtfully, then suddenly glanced up, laughing
with all the witchery at her command.

"Then, my dear American," she said insinu-
atingly, "I fear that you are going to refuse me
a very great favor."

"I hope not," Dan replied, gallantly.

"There is," pursued the Countess, "such a
thing as luck. Often a prophecy of that luck is
to be seen in one's face. I see such luck written
in your face now. Since you will not play for
yourself, I had hoped that you would be willing
to let me have the benefit of a little of the luck
that is so plainly written on your face. I had
hoped, up to this instant, that you would consent
to play as my proxy."

The Countess was looking at him in a way that
would have melted many a man into agreeing
to her wishes, but Dan answered promptly:

"I regret, Countess, to be compelled to refuse your request, but I would not play for myself, nor for anyone else."

"If you so detest Monte Carlo and its pursuits," replied the Countess with a pout, "I cannot understand why you are here."

"There was something useful to be gained from witnessing the sights here, but I have seen as much as I wish," Dalzell went on, "and now I am ready to leave. I am returning to my ship as soon as Darrin is ready to go."

"And he, also, is tired of Monte Carlo?" asked Countess Ripoli.

"Darrin's views are much the same as my own," Dan responded quietly.

Countess Ripoli bit her lip, then surveyed Dalzell with a sidelong look which she did not believe he saw, but Dan, trained in habits of observation, had missed nothing.

"Will you take me back to the tables?" asked the Countess suddenly.

"With pleasure," bowed Dan.

Lightly resting a hand on his arm the Countess guided Dalzell rather than walked with him. Back into the largest salon they moved.

Dan's eye roved about in search of Darrin, but that young ensign was not in sight.

At that very moment, in fact, Dave Darrin

was very much concerned in a matter upon which he had stumbled.

A few moments before his quick eye had espied Emil Gortchky crossing the room at a distance. Gortchky paused barely more than a few seconds to say a few words to a white-bearded, rather distinguished-looking foreigner. The older man returned Gortchky's look, then smiled slightly and moved on.

It was a trivial incident, but it was sufficient to set Dave's mind to working swiftly, on account of what he already knew about Mr. Green Hat.

For a few moments longer Ensign Darrin stood where he was; then, tiring of the scene, and wondering what had become of Danny Grin, he moved out upon one of the verandas, strolling slowly along. Reaching a darker part of the veranda, where a clump of small potted trees formed a toy grove, Dave paused, looking past the trees out upon the vague glimpses to be had of the Mediterranean by night.

There, in the near distance, gleamed the lights of the "Hudson." Darrin's face glowed with pride in the ship and in the Nation that stood behind her.

Almost unconsciously he stepped inside the little grove. For a few minutes longer his gaze rested on the sea. Then, hearing voices faintly, he turned to see if Dalzell were approaching.

Instead, it was the white-bearded foreigner, the murmur of whose voice had reached him. With him was another man, younger, black-haired, and with a face that somehow made the beholder think of an eagle.

The two men were engaged in close, low-voiced conversation.

"I'd better step into view," reflected Darrin, "so that they may not talk of private matters in my hearing."

Just then a chuckle escaped the younger of the pair, and with it Dave distinguished the word, "American."

It was the sneering intonation given the word that made Dave Darrin start slightly.

"Those men are discussing my country," muttered the young ensign, swiftly, "and one of them at least is well acquainted with that spy, Gortchky. Perhaps I shall do better to remain where I am."

Nor had Dave long to deliberate on this point, for the pair now neared the grove. They were speaking French, and in undertones, but Dave's ear was quick for that tongue, and he caught the words:

"England's friendship is important to America at the present moment, and it is very freely given, too. The English believe in their Yankee cousins."

"When the English lose a naval ship or two at Malta or elsewhere, and learn that it is the Americans who sink their ships, and then lie about it, will the English love for America be as great?" laughed the younger man.

"The English will be furious," smiled the white-bearded man, "and they will never learn the truth, either. For a hundred years to come Great Britain will hate the United States with the fiercest hatred."

"It is a desperate trick, but a clever one," declared the younger man, admiringly. "Nor will there be any way for either England or America to learn the truth. The whole world will know that the Yankees destroyed two British ships with all on board. It will probably bring the two countries to actual war. No matter though England is at present engaged in a huge war, the sentiment of her people would force her to take the United States on, too."

Ensign Dave Darrin, overhearing that conversation, and well knowing that he was listening to more than vaporing, felt his face blanch. He steeled himself to rigid posture as he felt himself trembling slightly.

Farther down the veranda strolled the French-speaking pair, then wheeled out of sight.

In a twinkling Dave strode silently, swiftly toward the salon that he had left. As he stepped into the brighter light, with admirable control, he slowed down to a sauntering stroll, looking smilingly about as though his whole mind were on the scenes of gambling before him.

A moment or two later Darrin's eyes caught sight of Dan Dalzell, as that young officer bowed the Countess Ripoli to a seat.

In vain did the Countess use her prettiest smiles to hold Danny Grin by her side as she played. Dalzell had been schooled at Annapolis and in the Navy itself, and knew how to take his leave gracefully, which he did, followed by the pouts of the Countess. As soon as she saw that the ensign's back was turned, a very unpleasant frown crossed her beautiful face.

Dave continued his stroll until he met Dan at a point where none stood near them.

"Keep on smiling, Dan," urged Dave, in an undertone. "Don't let that grin leave your face. But it's back to the ship for us on the double-quick! I may be dreaming, but I think I have found out the meaning of Mr. Green Hat's strange activities. I believe there is a plot on foot to bring England and our country into war with each other. One thing is certain. It's my duty to get back on board as fast as possible. I must tell the admiral what I have overheard."

Dan did not forget the injunction to keep on smiling. He proved so excellent an actor that he laughed heartily as Dave Darrin finished his few but thrilling words.

"Tiresome here, isn't it?" murmured Dan, aloud. "We might as well go back on board ship."

CHAPTER VII

THE ADMIRAL UNLOADS HIS MIND

REPORTING their coming aboard to the officer of the deck, Dave and Dan hastened to their respective quarters.

While Ensign Dalzell performed a "lightning change" from "cits" to uniform, Dave first seated himself at his desk, where he wrote a note hurriedly.

This done, he passed the word for an orderly, who promptly appeared.

"Take this note to the Captain," ordered Darrin.

"Aye, aye, sir," said the messenger.

Dave then hastened to make the necessary change in his own apparel. So quickly did he act, that he had his uniform on and was buttoning his blouse when the messenger returned.

"The Captain will see Ensigns Darrin and Dalzell immediately," reported the orderly.

Returning the orderly's salute, Dave buckled on his sword belt, hung on his sword, drew on his

white gloves, and started. He found his chum
ready.

Together the young officers reported at the
Captain's quarters. Captain Allen was already
seated at his desk.

"Orderly!" called the commanding officer
briskly.

"Aye, aye, sir."

"Guard the door and report that I am engaged."

"Aye, aye, sir."

In an instant Captain Allen, who had briefly
greeted his youngest officers, turned to them.

"Your note, Mr. Darrin, stated that you had a
matter to report to me of such importance that
you did not believe I would wish to lose a moment
in hearing what Mr. Dalzell and yourself could
tell me."

"That is the case, sir," Dave bowed. "Have
I your permission to proceed, sir?"

"Yes. You may take seats, if you wish."

Bowing their thanks, the young officers remained
on their feet.

Ensign Dave plunged at once into the narration of what had befallen them ashore.

Captain Allen listened to the tale without com-
ment, but when Dave related what he had overheard the two men say when passing the imitation
grove on the darkest part of the Casino veranda,
the commanding officer sprang to his feet.

"Mr. Darrin," he demanded, "are you positive of the words that you have just repeated?"

"I am, sir. In a matter of such importance I was careful to record every word in my mind just as it was uttered."

"Then I must communicate with the Admiral at once," continued Captain Allen, seating himself again. "Even if the Admiral be abed I consider this a subject of enough importance to call him."

Taking down the receiver of the telephone that led direct to the fleet commander's quarters, the Captain sent in a call to the Admiral's quarters.

Soon there came a response.

"This is the Captain speaking, Admiral," announced the "Hudson's" commanding officer. "Although the hour is late, sir, I request permission to report to you on a matter of importance."

"I will see you, Captain, in five minutes."

"Thank you, sir. I request permission to bring two officers with me."

"Permission is granted, Captain."

"Thank you, sir."

Hanging up the transmitter, Captain Allen sank back in his chair.

"Is there anything else, gentlemen, that you wish to say to me before we go to the Admiral?"

"I think I have told you all, sir," Dave replied.

"And I, too," Dalzell added.

Keeping his eye on the clock, Captain Allen presently arose, girded on his sword, parted the curtains, and led the way.

"If I am wanted, Orderly, I shall be in the Admiral's quarters."

"Aye, aye, sir."

The three officers then filed rapidly along the deck, presented themselves at the Admiral's quarters, and were admitted.

Admiral Timworth was standing at the rear of his cabin when the subordinate officers entered. He came quickly forward, instructed his orderly to guard the door, then turned to his visitors.

"I believe it will be best, with your permission, sir," began Captain Allen, "to let Mr. Darrin make his report to you."

"Mr. Darrin will proceed, then."

So Dave repeated the story he had told the Captain. Admiral Timworth listened until the recital had been finished, and then asked several questions.

"It does not sound like a hoax," commented Admiral Timworth, at last. "Yet it is impossible for me to conceive how two British battleships are to be sunk near Malta, or near anywhere else, and Americans blamed for the act. Captain Allen, can you imagine any way in which such a thing might be effected?"

"I cannot, sir."

"The subject must be given careful thought," declared the Admiral. "By the way, Mr. Darrin, do you think you could identify those two men who talked of the proposed destruction of the British battleships?"

"I am positive that I could do so, sir," Dave rejoined, "provided they were not disguised."

"Then you may meet them again, as we shall stop at various Mediterranean ports. If you do, sir, I wish you to report to me anything that you may find out about them. Mr. Dalzell did not see them, did he?"

"I may have passed them, sir," Dan replied, "but I would not know them, if meeting them, as the men whom Mr. Darrin mentions."

"Then, Captain, you will see to it," directed the Admiral, "that Mr. Dalzell has shore leave whenever Mr. Darrin does. The two young men will go ashore together so that Mr. Darrin, if opportunity presents, may indicate the plotters to Mr. Dalzell."

The Captain and the young officers bowed their understanding of this order.

"The presence of Gortchky here, taken with what Mr. Darrin overheard those men talking about, and coupled with what took place on the mole at Gibraltar, leads me to believe that some foreign government has plans for involving the

United States government in serious complica-
tions," resumed the Admiral, after a pause.
"Gortchky is not in charge of any very extensive
plot. He is simply a tool of greater minds, and
it may easily be that the pair whom Mr. Darrin
overheard are those who are directing Gortchky in
some really big and dangerous scheme. By the
way, gentlemen, was either of you introduced to
any young or charming woman ashore?"

"We were both presented to the Countess
Ripoli, sir," Darrin answered, at once.

"And at the Countess's request, I took a little
turn with her on one of the verandas, sir," Dan
added.

"Tell me all about the Countess and your
meeting with her, Mr. Dalzell," Admiral Timworth directed.

So Dan plunged at once into a narration of his
chat with the Countess, to which Admiral Timworth listened attentively.

"Ripoli?" he mused aloud, at last. "I do not
recall the name as that of a supposed secret service
agent. Ripoli? Let me see."

From a drawer of his desk the Admiral drew
out an indexed book. He turned over, pre-
sumably, to the letter "R," then scanned the
writing on several pages.

"She has not been reported to me as a suspected
secret service agent of any country," said the fleet

commander, aloud. "Yet she may very likely be a spy in the service of some ring of international trouble-makers. I will enter her name now, though I cannot place anything positive against it."

"If either of us should meet the Countess Ripoli again, sir," queried Dan, "have you any orders, sir, in that event?"

"If you do meet her," replied the admiral, "do not be too distant with her, and do not let her see that she is in any sense under suspicion. Just treat her as you would any charming woman whom you might meet socially. However, should you meet her again, you may report the fact to me. I shall doubtless have some further instructions for you, gentlemen, but that is all for the present. Captain, you will remain."

Formally saluting their superiors, Dave and Dan withdrew and returned to Dave's quarters. For half an hour Dan remained chatting with Dave, then went to his own quarters.

By daylight the "Hudson" was under way again, bound for Naples. Dan and Dave were called to stand their watches, and life on the battleship went on as usual.

It was but an hour after daylight when Admiral Timworth, who had remained up the rest of the night with Flag Lieutenant Simpson, sent a long message to the Navy Department at Washington.

The message crackled out over the "Hudson's" wireless aerials, and was soon afterward received in Washington at the huge naval wireless station there.

"Good night, Simpson," said the Admiral, when his flag lieutenant reported that the message was in the hands of the wireless operator.

"Shall I leave any instructions for your being called, sir?" asked Lieutenant Simpson.

"Have me called at ten o'clock, unless a reply from the Navy Department should arrive earlier. In that case have me called at once."

The flag lieutenant is the personal aide of the fleet commander.

If the Admiral received an interesting reply from the Navy Department during the voyage to Naples, he at least concealed the fact from Ensigns Darrin and Dalzell. Ensigns, however, are quite accustomed to reserve on the part of admirals.

It was one o'clock one sunny afternoon when the "Hudson" entered the Bay of Naples. Her anchorage having already been assigned by wireless by the port authorities at Naples, the "Hudson" came to anchor close to the "Kennebec" and "Lowell" of the Mediterranean Fleet. Admiral Timworth now had three war vessels under his own eyes.

At four bells (two o'clock) an orderly called

at Dan's and Dave's quarters, with orders to report to the Admiral at once.

When the two young ensigns reached the Admiral's quarters they found Lieutenant Simpson there also.

"Be seated, gentlemen," directed the Admiral.

For a few moments Admiral Timworth shuffled papers on his desk, glancing briefly at some of them.

"Now, gentlemen," said the Admiral, wheeling about in his chair and looking impressively at Darrin and Dalzell, "it seems to me I had better preface my remarks by giving you some idea of the Fleet's unusual and special mission in the Mediterranean. That may lead you to a better comprehension of why a certain foreign power should wish to create, between Great Britain and the United States, a situation that would probably call for war between the two greatest nations of the world."

CHAPTER VIII

ON LIVELY SPECIAL DUTY

IN the first place," resumed the Admiral, "you must know that relations between Great Britain and the United States are, and for some time have been, of an especially cordial nature. Throughout the great war Great Britain has been compelled to buy a large part of her food and munitions in the United States. Except for her being able to do so she would have been forced out of the war and the Entente Allies would have been defeated. There are Englishmen who will make you feel that the saving force of the United States is greatly appreciated in England, just as there are other Englishmen who will remark stupidly that the United States as a seller, has had a great opportunity to grow rich at England's expense.

"There can be no doubt that thinking Englishmen are prepared to go to almost any extent to cultivate and keep the friendship of the United States, just as duller-witted Englishmen declare that the United States depends upon England for existence.

"During the present war Great Britain has felt compelled to impose certain blockade restrictions upon our commerce with neutral powers in Europe. This has hampered our commerce to some extent, and there are many in the United States who feel deep resentment, and favor taking any steps necessary to compel England to abandon her interference with our merchant marine. Some Englishmen take an almost insolent attitude in the matter, while others beg us to believe that England hinders some of our commerce only in order to preserve her own national life. In other words, if she did not carefully regulate the world's trade with, for instance, Denmark and Holland, those countries would sell much of their importations to Germany, whereby the duration of the war would be prolonged by reason of help obtained by Germany in that manner.

"As you can readily understand, the situation is full of delicate points, and many sensibilities are wounded. There have been times when only a spark was needed to kindle a serious blaze of mutual wrath between Great Britain and the United States. And you may be sure there are some governments in this world that would be delighted to see feelings of deep hostility engendered between Britons and Americans.

"At present, however, there seems to be not the slightest cloud over the relations between Great Britain and our country.

"Now, Mr. Darrin, you have obtained clues to a startling plot that has for its object the causing of distrust between the two greatest nations. If one or more British warships should be sunk, by some means that we do not at present know, and if the blame could be plausibly laid against Americans, there would be hot-tempered talk in England and a lot of indignant retort from our country. It would seem preposterous that any Englishman could suspect the American government of destroying British warships, and just as absurd to think that Americans could take such a charge seriously. Yet in the relations between nations the absurd thing often does happen. Should England lose any warships it would seem that only Germany or Austria could be blamed, yet it might be possible for plotters to manage the thing so successfully, and with so much cleverness, that the United States would really seem to be proven to be the guilty party. Our duty as officers of the Navy can be performed only by frustrating the hideous plot altogether.

"So, Ensigns Darrin and Dalzell, while we are at Naples you will spend as much of your time as possible on shore. You will go about everywhere, as though to see the sights of the city and as if bent on getting your fill of pleasure. Unless under pressing need you will not be extravagant in your expenditures, but will conduct yourselves as though sight-seeing within the limits of your modest pay as ensigns. You will, however, not be put to any expense in the matter, as all your expenditures will be returned to you out of an emergency fund in my hands.

"Your object in going ashore will be to report if you see Gortchky in Naples. I feel rather certain that the fellow is already there. You, Mr. Darrin, will also keep your eyes wide open for a sight of either or both of that pair whom you overheard talking at Monte Carlo. You will also note and report if you find the Countess Ripoli in Naples."

"And if we meet her and if she speaks to us, sir?" asked Dalzell. "What if she even wishes to entertain us, or to claim our escort?"

"Do whatever you can to please the Countess," replied the Admiral, promptly. "Be agreeable to her in any way that does not interfere with other and more important duties to which I have assigned you."

Judging by a sign from the fleet commander that the interview was now at an end, Dave and Dan rose, standing at attention.

"Perhaps I have given you a wrong impression in one particular," Admiral Timworth continued. "I do not wish you to understand, gentlemen, that I have intimated that any power, or any combination of powers, has directly ordered any act that would lead to the sinking of British warships. Governments, even the worst, do not act in that way. The thing which the power I have in mind may have done is to give certain secret agents a free hand to bring about war between England and the United States. Undoubtedly, the secret agents at the bottom of this conspiracy have been left free to choose their own methods. Thus the foreign government interested in this conspiracy could feel that it did not *order* the commission of a crime, no matter what might happen as the result. Now, gentlemen, have you any questions to ask?"

"None, sir," Dave Darrin responded immediately.

"None, sir," echoed Dalzell.

"Then you may go," rejoined Admiral Timworth, rising and returning the parting salutes of the young officers.

It was presently noised about among the ship's company that Ensigns Darrin and Dalzell had been ordered ashore on special duty.

"How did you work it?" Lieutenant Barnes irritably demanded of Danny Grin.

"Why? Do you want to work a trick yourself?" asked Dalzell, unsympathetically.

"No such luck for me," growled Barnes. "While in port I am ordered to take charge of shifting stores below decks."

"Fine!" approved Dan.

"And I wish I had you for junior officer on that detail," growled Barnes.

"If I get tired of staying ashore," Danny Grin proposed genially, "I'll make humble petition to be assigned as junior on your detail."

CHAPTER IX

M. DALNY PLANS A TRAGEDY

SAY, I wonder if these people call this a square deal," muttered Danny Grin, as he surveyed the dish that the waiter had just left for him. "I called for ham and eggs and potatoes, and the fellow has brought me chicken and this dish of vegetables that none but a native could name."

"Call the waiter back and ask him to explain his mistake," Ensign Darrin suggested, smilingly.

"I can't talk their lingo," returned Dalzell plaintively.

"Nor can I speak much of it, either," admitted Dave.

"Can you speak any Italian?"

"Only a little, and very badly at that."

"Where did you learn Italian?" demanded Danny Grin.

"From an Italian-American cook on board our ship," Darrin explained.

"Whew! You must have done that while I was asleep," Dalzell complained.

"I don't know enough Italian to carry me very far," laughed Darrin. "Perhaps between two and three hundred useful words, and some of the parts of a few verbs. Let me see just what you thought you were ordering."

Dan held out a somewhat soiled bill of fare on which the names of the dishes were printed in Italian and English.

"I tried to pronounce the Italian words right," Dan went on, with a grimace.

"Let me hear you read the words over again," Dave begged.

Dan did so, his comrade's smile deepening.

"Dan," said Dave dryly, "you speak Italian as though it were French. Italian is too delicate a language for that treatment."

"But what am I to do about this chicken?" Danny Grin persisted.

"Eat it," suggested Darrin, "and use some of your time ashore in getting closer to the Italian language."

Dave was served with just what he had ordered for a pleasing meal — an omelet, spaghetti and Neapolitan tomatoes, with dessert to follow.

"I'm no great admirer of chicken, and I did want ham," sighed Dan, as he glanced enviously at his chum's dainty food. Nevertheless Ensign Dalzell ate his meal with an air of resignation that greatly amused Dave Darrin.

The restaurant was one of the largest and handsomest to be found along that great thoroughfare of Naples, the Riviera di Chiaja. The place would seat perhaps four hundred guests. At this hour of the day there were about half that number of persons present, many of whom were Americans.

The chums had succeeded in obtaining a small table by themselves, close to an open window that overlooked the sidewalk.

Watching the throngs that passed, both on foot and in carriages of many types, the young naval officers felt certain that at no other point could they obtain as good a general view of the city of Naples. Many well-to-do Italians were afoot, having sold their carriages and automobiles in order to buy the war bonds of their country. As there were several Italian warships in port, sailors from these craft were ashore and mingling with the throng. Soldiers home on sick leave from the Austrian frontier were to be seen. Other men, who looked like mere lads, wore new army uniforms proudly. These latter were the present year's recruits, lately called to the colors and drilling for the work that lay ahead of them, work in deadly earnest against hated Austria.

All that went on before the café was interesting enough. It was not, however, until near the end of the meal that anything happened of personal interest to Dave and Dan.

Then there was a quick step behind them, next a voice cried gaily:

"My dear Monsieur Darrin, who could have expected to see you here?"

"Any one who knew that my ship is in the harbor might have expected to see me here," replied Dave, rising and smiling. "How do you do, Monsieur le Comte?"

It was indeed the Count of Surigny, and that dapper, well-set-up young Frenchman was nattily dressed, smiling, and with an unmistakable air of prosperity about him.

Dan had also risen. Then as the three seated themselves Dave inquired what refreshment his friend of Monte Carlo would allow them the pleasure of ordering for him. The Count asked only for a cup of coffee, after which the chat went merrily on.

"My dear Darrin, I rejoice to be able to tell you that I have determined never again to visit Monte Carlo," said the Count. "Moreover, I am prosperous and happy. Ah, what a debt of gratitude I owe you! I know you must be wondering why I am not serving my country in the trenches."

"I knew you must have some good reason for not serving in the French army at such a time," Dave replied.

"I tried to enter the army," Surigny replied,

"but the surgeons refused to pass me. One of my eyes is too weak, and there is, besides, some little irregularity in the action of my heart that would make it impossible for me to endure the hardships of a soldier. So, despite my protests and entreaties, the surgeons have refused to accept me for military service."

"Is it permitted to ask if you have found employment?" Dave inquired.

"I have found employment of a sort," the Count rattled on, without a shade of embarrassment. "It might be questioned if I am worth the remuneration which I receive, but at least I am happy. I am permitted to serve a friend in some little matters of a personal nature."

That answer was enough to prevent Dave from making any further inquiries as to the Count's new means of a livelihood.

"It gives me the greatest happiness to be able to see you again, and to hear your voice," continued the Count. "I am here in Naples only as a matter of accident, and it may be that my stay here will be short. I was at a table in the rear with a friend when I espied you sitting here. Is it permitted that I bring my friend over and present him?"

"We shall be delighted to meet any friend of yours, Surigny," Dave replied pleasantly.

"Then I shall bring him here at once," replied

the Frenchman, lightly, rising and moving rapidly
away.

"I wonder what line of work the Count can be
in now," mused Dalzell, aloud. "It would appear to be something that pays him very well and
allows him to travel. I wonder if the friend he
is to introduce to us is the one that employs him."

"We shall know that if Count Surigny chooses
to inform us," smiled Dave.

Then their talk ceased, for they heard the
Count's voice in conversation with some one as
he came up behind them.

"My dear Monsieur Darrin," cried the Count,
"I am honored in being able to present to you
Monsieur Dalny."

Ensign Darrin rose, wheeled and thrust out
his hand. Then his eyes turned to the new-
comer's face.

Nor could the young naval officer repress a
slight start, for M. Dalny was unmistakably one
of the two men whom he had overheard on the
veranda of the Casino at Monte Carlo.

"Monsieur Darrin," replied M. Dalny, ac-
cepting Dave's hand, "I feel that I am indeed
honored in being able to meet one who, I understand, has been such a friend to my friend the
Count of Surigny. I shall hope to see much of
you."

Dalny was then introduced to Dalzell, after

which, at Dave's invitation, the newcomers seated themselves. Fresh coffee was ordered.

But Dave Darrin's head was now in a good deal of a whirl.

As to the identity of M. Dalny, there could be no mistake whatever. And here was the Count of Surigny, evidently in the friendship of this plotter against the American Navy. It was not unlikely that the Count, too, was in the employ of this enemy of the United States.

"What can this whole thing mean, and does Surigny *know* that he is working against the peace and honor of my country?" Dave asked himself, his pulses throbbing.

"Are you to be here long at Naples, Monsieur Darrin?" Dalny soon asked in his most velvet-like tones.

"I really haven't the least idea, Monsieur Dalny," Dave replied truthfully, forcing a smile. "I am not deep in the confidence of Admiral Timworth."

"I thought it very likely," purred Monsieur Dalny, "that you might have heard from your officers as to how many days of shore liberty are likely to be granted your sailors."

"Oh, probably we shall —" began Dan, who found the French conversation easy to understand in this instance.

But the slightest of signs from Darrin was

sufficient to check Dalzell's intended statement. So Danny Grin merely finished:

"Probably we shall hear soon how long our stay here is to be."

"Are you interested, Monsieur Dalny, in the length of our stay here?" queried Ensign Dave, gazing carelessly into the eyes of the stranger.

"Oh, it is but a matter of idle curiosity to me," replied the other, shrugging his shoulders amiably. "Just as you understand it would be a matter of a little curiosity, my dear Monsieur Darrin, to know whether the American fleet now in the harbor here will keep together for the next few weeks, and what ports you will visit. But I imagine that you have, as yet, no information on such points."

Dave did not reply to M. Dalny's remarks, who, however, did not appear to notice the omission. Drawing forth a long cigar and lighting it, Dalny puffed away, seeming to prefer, after that, to listen to the conversation of the others.

"Who can this Monsieur Dalny be?" Dave asked himself, racking his brain. "And of what nationality? The word 'Monsieur' is French in itself, though Dalny is hardly a French name. Perhaps it makes little difference, though, for men who sell their time and services as I am afraid this Dalny fellow is doing, are quite likely to masquerade under assumed names."

Presently M. Dalny excused himself for a few moments. Sauntering toward the rear of the restaurant, he stepped into a side passage, then made a quick entrance into a private room, the door of which he instantly locked. He now crossed the room and stood before the solitary diner in that room.

"My dear Mender!" cried Dalny.

"Your face betrays interest, Dalny," remarked the other, who was the older of the pair whom Dave had heard on the Casino veranda.

"And I am interested," continued Dalny, in a low tone. "I have met the two young officers from the American flagship."

"That is what you are here to do," smiled Monsieur Mender.

"The fellow Darrin refuses me any information about the movements of the American fleet."

"That was perhaps to be expected," answered Mender reflectively.

"But I fear matters are worse than that," Dalny went on hurriedly.

"Explain yourself, Dalny."

"Darrin did not see my face until he rose to greet me, when Surigny introduced us," continued Dalny. "Then he started, slightly, yet most plainly. Monsieur Mender, that young American naval officer knows something about us."

"Not very likely, Dalny."

"Then he at least suspects something."

"Why should he?"

"Monsieur Mender," hurried on Dalny, "you recall that evening on the Casino veranda at Monte Carlo? You and I, as we approached a little grove of potted trees, talked rather more incautiously than we should have done."

"It was an indiscretion, true," nodded the white-haired Mender thoughtfully.

"And, afterwards, as you know, I told you I thought I heard someone move behind those little trees."

"And so —?"

"I suspect, Monsieur Mender, that it was Ensign Darrin, of the battleship 'Hudson,' who stood behind those trees, and who overheard us."

"I wish I knew if such were the case," replied M. Mender huskily, his face paling with anxiety.

"If Darrin overheard our talk, he doubtless reported it to his superior officers," declared Dalny.

"Unquestionably — if he really heard," admitted Mender.

"Then that pair of young officers, for they are close friends, must have been sent ashore to see if they could get track of the numerous party whom you direct, my dear Monsieur Mender."

"You believe that the two young American officers are ashore in Naples as spies upon us?" questioned Mender, his tone cold and deadly.

"It would seem so," Dalny answered readily.

"In that case —" began Mender, slowly, then paused.

"In that case — what?" demanded Dalny, after waiting a few moments while his chief reflected.

"It would mean that the Italian authorities, as soon as informed of what is suspected against us, would send out their keenest men to locate us, and then we should be arrested."

"What could be done to us?" queried Dalny.

"In these war days not very much evidence is required against men who are accused of being spies, my excellent Dalny. We might or we might not be accorded a trial, but one thing is quite sure; we would be shot to death on the charge of being spies."

As he pronounced these significant words Mender shrugged his shoulders. His manner was cool, one would have said almost unconcerned.

"You are right," agreed the younger plotter. "The Italians, like all the other peoples engaged in this war, hate spies bitterly, and would be quick to mete out death to us."

"It would be desirable," Mender proceeded, "to prevent the young officers from going back aboard their ship."

"How?" asked Dalny, bluntly.

Mender laughed, cold-bloodedly, in a low tone.

"In Naples," he explained, "there are, as you know, my dear Dalny, hundreds of bravos, some of whom are the most desperate fellows in the world — men who would stick at nothing to earn a few *lira*. And they will ask no awkward questions as to which country they serve in aiding us."

"Then you would have Darrin and Dalzell seized, by night, by some of these bravos, and carried away to a secure place where they could be confined until your plans have been carried through?" inquired Dalny, thoughtfully.

"It is always dangerous to have banditti seize men and hide them away, especially in a country that is engaged in war," replied Mender, slowly. "Now, if, in one of the narrow, dark streets of Old Naples, these young Americans were settled by a few quiet thrusts with the blade, their bodies might then be dropped into a sewer. The bodies might not be found for weeks. On the other hand, captives, no matter how securely hidden, may find means to escape, and all our care in the matter would go for naught. Besides, these Sicilian bravos of Naples much prefer to settle a man with one or two quick thrusts with a narrow blade, and then — But what is the matter, Dalny? Does the use of the knife terrify you?"

"No!" replied Dalny, huskily. "I was merely

thinking that, if a man like either Darrin or Dalzell escaped from a knife, after seeing its flash,
and if he suspected me of being behind the attempt, either young man would be likely to lay
hold of me and snap my spine."

"If you are fearful of the chances and of the
possible consequences, Dalny," replied Mender
coldly, "you may withdraw."

"No, no, no!" protested Dalny quickly. "You
are my chief, Monsieur Mender, and whatever
you wish I shall do."

Mender puffed for a few moments at a Russian
cigarette, before he again spoke.

"Dalny," he said, "you may be sure I do not
distrust either your loyalty or your courage.
Go back to your Americans. Detain them as
long as needful at the table, no matter by what
arts. Within twenty minutes I shall have a
leader of Neapolitan bravos here, and I shall
have a plan to unfold to him. Then he will go
and post his men. You will receive instructions
from me that you cannot mistake. You are
right in fearing Darrin and Dalzell. We can
afford to take no chances. That pair of young
American officers shall have no chance of reporting our presence in Naples to their superior
officers. Sooner than permit the least risk of
interference with our plans I shall remove them
from our way."

"Darrin and Dalzell are to be killed, then?" asked Dalny hoarsely.

"They shall be snuffed out," replied Mender, flicking the ash from his cigarette. "Go, Dalny, and do your part as far as you have heard it from me. I will attend to the rest. Do not be uneasy."

Dalny made a low bow before his cold-blooded chief, then left the private room, returning to Ensigns Darrin and Dalzell, whose death, under the knives of cowardly treachery, he must do his best to help bring about!

CHAPTER X

TREACHERY HAS THE FLOOR

YOU will not have much time for sight-seeing, I am afraid," Count Surigny was saying, as Monsieur Dalny soft-footedly returned to the table.

"I do not know how much time we shall have," Dave answered.

"If you have but little time, then it will be most unfortunate," spoke Dalny softly, with his engaging smile. "Naples is vastly rich in things that are worth while seeing."

"We are not likely to have the time to see many of them," Darrin answered.

"That is most unfortunate," replied the Count, in a regretful tone.

"Yet there is a way to partly overcome that misfortune," suggested Mr. Dalny.

"How, Monsieur?" inquired Darrin, turning his gaze on the face of the international plotter.

"Why, secure a good guide, engage a carriage drawn by good horses, and then move from point to point as fast as possible," replied Dalny. "I know Naples well. Perhaps I can offer my services for, say, this evening."

"Are the public places of interest likely to be open in the evening?" questioned Dave.

"Not the museums," admitted M. Dalny. "But there are many other things to be seen. Naples has several beautiful parks. Some of them contain notable statues. These parks are the nightly resort of all classes of the Italian community, who are always worth observing. Then, too, there are many curious glimpses to be had of the night life of the underworld of Naples. In a word, Monsieur Darrin, there are enough night sights, of one kind and another, to fill profitably a month in Naples. And, as I know the city, you may command me. I will be your guide. Shall we go to-night?"

"Where could we go, with the most advantage in the matter of sight-seeing?" Dave asked.

"Out toward Vomero," suggested young Count Surigny.

"Too fashionable, and very dull," replied Dalny, with a shake of his head.

"Then where?" asked Dan.

But Dalny's reply was lost to him, for at that moment Darrin, holding a rolled napkin at one side of the table, and below the level of the table top, waved it slowly back and forth. Dan was the only one of the party at the table who could see the moving napkin. By this simple wig-wag signal device Dave Darrin sent to his chum the silent message:

"Dalny is one of the plotters I overheard on the Casino veranda. Think he suspects us. Follow my lead."

The instant that the message ended Dan glanced slowly around him, then upward at the ceiling.

Soon Dalny's interest in the table talk waned for outside on the sidewalk he caught sight of a young Neapolitan dandy, standing on the curb, his back turned to the restaurant as he swung a jaunty little cane. The motions of that cane spelled out a message that only Dalny, of all the party at the table, could read. And that message read:

"Get carriage, take Americans for drive at dark. Finally, direct driver to turn into the Strada di Mara. Leave carriage with Americans when urged by shop-keeper."

That was the whole message. It was plain enough, however, to instruct Dalny as fully as he needed to be directed. The scoundrel, as he watched the swinging movements of the cane, looked out into the street between half-closed eyelids, slowly puffing out rings of smoke from his long cigar.

"We are becoming dull, good friends," laughed Dalny presently, glancing at the others. "Suppose we order more coffee."

"No more for me, thank you," protested Dave.

"But you have had hardly any coffee," Dalny declared.

"I am ready to admit that I can't keep up with the average American in drinking coffee," Dave replied.

"But you will have more, my dear Dalzell," urged Dalny.

Dan, who was inwardly agitated over the information he had received secretly from his chum, looked at Dalny almost with a start. In Dan's soul there was loathing for this foreigner with the engaging smile.

"I do not believe I can stand any more coffee," confessed Dan.

"So you and I, Surigny, must drink all the coffee at this table," said Dalny, with a shrug of his shoulders.

"I can drink a little more," replied the Count.

The day was now rapidly waning, bringing on a balminess of evening such as is found in few places other than Naples. The streets were becoming crowded with pedestrians.

"Waiter," called Dalny, "you will be good enough to secure for us a carriage with good horses. Get it as quickly as you can."

But the waiter, perceiving a signal from Dalny, knew that the carriage must not arrive too soon.

In the meantime Dave scanned the bill that

had been presented for the meal, then laid a banknote on the bill. The waiter, returning, attended to the paying of the bill and received his "tip" from the change that he brought back.

The party lingered at the table to wait for the arrival of the carriage that was intended to convey Dave Darrin and Dan Dalzell to their death.

"My dear Count," said Dalny presently, "I regret much that the appointment which you told me you had for this evening will prevent you from going with us. Can you not manage to break the appointment without doing injustice to others?"

Taking his cue from the manner in which the question was put, the Comte of Surigny replied:

"It would delight me beyond measure to be one of the party to-night, but it is impossible. My appointment cannot be set aside."

The restaurant was brilliantly lighted, and the street lights had begun to flash out as the carriage arrived.

"Now, for a night of real sight-seeing!" cried Dalny, rising eagerly. "My dear Americans, I promise you something such as you have never before experienced!"

"I am heartily sorry that you are prevented from going with us, Surigny," declared Dave, holding out his hand to the young Frenchman.

"I shall pray for better fortune next time," smiled the Count, rather sadly.

"We are all desolate that you cannot go with us, Surigny," declared Dalny, also holding out his hand. Dan, too, shook hands with Surigny. Then the international plotter led the two Americans to the carriage awaiting outside.

After the Count of Surigny had waved his hand to the party and had walked away, Dalny placed Dave and Dan on the rear seat of the barouche, while he himself sat facing them.

A few words in Italian from Dalny, and the horses started. For half an hour the driver took his fares past ordinary sights.

"But we are not much interested, driver," cried Dalny, turning at last to the man who held the lines. "We are bored with this dullness, when Naples holds so much that may be seen by night. Take us through the Strada di Mara."

So the driver headed his horses toward the eastern, or older, part of the city. The Strada di Mara leads through one of the most thickly populated sections of Naples, and a part of the street extends up a steep hillside.

"You see how poor the people are here," said Dalny, as the horses slowed down to a walk. "We shall come soon, however, to a more interesting part of the street. Crime lurks here, also; not the more desperate crimes though. The Strada di Mara, in one part, is the resort of thieves who wish to dispose of their petty plunder by turning it into cash. And, as strange merchandise is dealt in here, the shops offer a variety of wares. We will presently look into one or two of the shops."

"What on earth can Dalny be driving at?" wondered young Ensign Darrin. "Can he think that we would enter such shops, and buy the plunder that thieves have sold there?"

At the next street corner an Italian lad with a sweet voice began to sing. Danny Grin noticed that most of the people in this steep, narrow alley, that was by courtesy called a street, were now going indoors. Only a man here and there remained outside.

"That's curious," thought Dan to himself. "Don't these people like music, that a street singer should drive them inside?"

When the carriage had passed on to the next block a man came out of a shop and waved his hand to the driver, who promptly reined in his horses.

"Gentlemen," urged the shop-keeper, in English, "be kind enough to step inside and look at some of the bargains I am offering."

Dave, who understood, whispered to Dalny:

"It can hardly be worth while to get out and look at what is probably stolen goods."

"On the contrary," rejoined Dalny, "this man is likely to show us some things that will help me in explaining the interesting points of Naples to you. Come!"

Opening the door of the carriage, the international plotter stepped out, leading the way. Of course Dave and Dan followed him.

It now turned out that the Italian's shop was some doors farther up along this block. As he led the way, and Dalny and the Americans followed, neither young officer observed that the driver had turned his horses around and was driving away.

At the same time, the few men now on the sidewalk of this block started to close in on the little party.

Tragedy was stepping across the threshold!

CHAPTER XI

HEMMED IN BY THE BRAVOS

SUDDENLY out of a doorway lurched a big Sicilian, seemingly intoxicated.

He lurched against Dave, then drew back, scowling fiercely at the young ensign.

"Your mistake, sir," spoke Darrin, purposely using English.

Dave would have passed, but now the fellow placed himself squarely in Darrin's way.

"You have struck me!" snarled the Sicilian in his own language. "Why?"

Then, uttering a peculiar cry, the man, with a movement of wonderful swiftness, drew a knife. In the dim light that blade flashed like subdued fire.

"One, two, three — out!" gritted Dave Darrin, leaping forward.

Striking up the fellow's arm, Dave caught at the knife-wrist. He twisted it savagely and the weapon clattered to the rough pavement.

Bump! Dave struck the fellow hard between the eyes, sending him to earth, where he lay still.

Dan, now keenly alert, discovered that the pretended shopkeeper had also drawn a knife.

"To quarters!" yelled Danny Grin.

"Back to back!" shouted Dave, placing his shoulders close to his chum's. "Dan, we must fight for our lives. The lives of all these cattle are not worth a scratch on our bodies! Down 'em!"

"We'll make ten-pins of 'em," hissed Dalzell.

And Monsieur Dalny? That honorable gentleman was now scuttling down the street to safety.

The fight that followed was a mixture of boxing, football tactics and sheer Yankee grit that Dave and Dan now employed as they faced more than half a dozen scoundrels armed with the long, thin knives of the bravos of Naples.

Bump! Ensign Darrin struck up the arm of the first scoundrel to reach for him. In a twinkling Dave had broken that rascal's right wrist, forcing the fellow to drop his weapon.

Like a flash Dave caught his victim up, holding him overhead and sending the bravo, heels first, into the face of another scoundrel. The man, struck by this human missile, went to earth dazed, and with a broken jaw to boot.

Dalzell, too, was proving the stuff that was in him. Dodging a descending hand that held a knife, then landing a smashing blow over the fellow's heart, Dan sent him to earth. At that instant a knife would have gone through Danny

Grin's ribs had not Dalzell let one of his feet fly
with such speed and skill as to break another
bravo's shin-bone.

Crouching low, Dave received still another
assailant. Seizing him below the knees, then
rising, he hurled the ruffian over backward on
his head, the fall nearly snapping the owner's
spine at the neck and leaving him unconscious.

Two more men were quickly downed, and seemed
inclined to stay there. The young ensigns had
not received a scratch so far, which was due as
much to luck as to their own skill.

Now a wail of terror rose on the air. Two of
the bravos took fairly to their heels. The rest
wavered, then gave way, glaring with sullen
looks at these young Americans who could fight
so terribly without weapons.

"Come on!" urged Dave, in a low voice. "Let's
get out of here! There is no credit in staying
here and taking on more fighting. Let's hurry
while the hurrying is good."

Only one of the bravos was ahead of them as
the young naval officers began their sprint. That
fellow was trying to get out of harm's way, but
hearing pursuit at his heels, the frightened fellow
halted suddenly, wheeled and struck out with
his knife at Ensign Darrin.

Dave dodged, then landed both fists against
the ruffian's ribs, knocking the fellow clean

through a window with a great crashing of glass.

"Hustle!" muttered Dalzell, as he halted to wait for his chum. "There may be a hundred more of these fellows who can be called out on a single block."

But there was no pursuit. The bravos had had enough. Afterwards it was a matter of local report that two of the rascals handled by Darrin and Dalzell all but died of their injuries. The Strada di Mara contained no bravos reckless enough to follow these incredible Americans on this wild night of trouble.

Still sprinting, Dave, with Dan at his heels, overhauled a running figure. Dave shot out his right hand, gathering in, by the coat collar, Monsieur Dalny.

"My friend," uttered Dave grimly, as he halted the fugitive, "this does not appear to be one of your best fighting nights."

"I — I — I —" stammered M. Dalny, his face white. "I — I —"

"So you said before," Dave retorted dryly. "Let it go at that."

"Do you mean to charge that I ran away?" demanded Dalny, with a show of injured dignity.

"Certainly not," retorted Dave, ironically. "You were merely trying to show two scared Americans the shortest way back to a safe part of Naples."

"It's not safe here," whispered Dalny, trembling. "We are almost certain to be followed by an enraged mob. Let us use discretion."

The word "discretion" recalled Darrin to the fact that he must not be too rough with the fellow through whom he hoped to learn something of great interest to Admiral Timworth.

"You are right, Monsieur Dalny," agreed the young ensign. "Let us waste little time in getting away from this part of Naples."

No walk could have been too brisk, just then, for Dalny. He was not a coward in all things, but he felt a deadly terror of cold steel.

In addition, this international plotter had, just then, a lively conviction that friends of the men whom these American officers had handled so roughly might, if they overtook him, feel a decided thirst for vengeance upon the man who had led such giants against the bravos of the Strada di Mara.

"Why are you looking back so often?" Dave asked, as the three gained the next corner.

"To see if we are pursued," confessed Dalny.

"That is prudent," Darrin smiled, "yet hardly necessary."

"What do you mean?" asked the international plotter.

"Because," explained Dan, grinning, "the only bravos who have any reason to be afraid

"Dave shot out his right hand."

of us to-night are those who might get in front of us. Those who keep behind us will have every chance to get away unharmed."

"You are a droll pair," muttered Dalny.

"And, unless I am greatly in error, my fine fellow, you led us into that trap for the purpose of having something bad happen us," muttered Dave, but he kept the words behind his teeth, for he did not care, as yet, to come to an open quarrel with this fellow.

Before long the three reached one of the broader, well-lighted thoroughfares. Here they engaged a driver and carriage, and were soon once more in the Riviera di Chiaja.

As they passed one of the larger buildings, Mender, looking down upon the avenue through the blinds of a window of a room at the hotel, saw the three as they drove past an arc light.

"What can be the matter with that simpleton Dalny?" muttered the arch-plotter. "Did he, at the last moment, fail in the courage necessary to lead the Americans into the trap that I had baited for them?"

Ten minutes later Dalny, closeted with his chief, was relating to that astounded leader the story of what had happened in the Strada di Mara.

"I cannot understand it," muttered Mender.

"No more can I," rejoined Dalny. "The

Americans are demons when it comes to fighting."

"At some point, my good Dalny, you must have bungled the affair."

"Why not say that the fault must have been with your choice of bravos?" jeered the subordinate. "Why did you pick out alleged bravos who would allow themselves to be put to flight by unarmed men?"

"I must wait until I have a fuller report of this night's misadventure," declared Mender. "I dare say that, within a few hours, I shall have more exact information."

In this belief Mender was quite right. Before daylight he was visited by the leader of the bravos of the Strada di Mara, who announced that he must be paid two thousand *lira* (about four hundred dollars) as extra money to be divided among his outraged followers.

In the case that this extra money was not forthcoming, declared the leader of the bravos, Mender and his friends might find Naples much too dangerous a city for them.

CHAPTER XII

EVIL EYES ON SAILORMAN RUNKLE

IN the center of a huge room in the Hotel dell'
Orso, overlooking the Chiaja, Dave Darrin
and Dalzell came to a halt.

Below they had just left Dalny in the carriage, and had come straight up to their room,
which they had engaged when first they came
ashore.

They had not, as one might suspect, overlooked
the opportunity of finding whither Dalny drove
after leaving them. For a short, broad-shouldered
young man, Able Seaman Runkle, U. S. S. "Hudson," had been on the lookout for them on the
sidewalk.

Runkle, by special order of Captain Allen,
U. S. N., was not in uniform, but in civilian
attire. In another carriage Able Seaman Runkle,
at Dave's order, followed the conveyance that
took Dalny back to the appointed meeting
place with Mender. The sailorman's carriage
did not, of course, stop when Dalny's vehicle
did, but kept slowly on.

"Shadowing" is often a two-edged tool. When

Runkle returned to his post he, in turn, was followed by the same dandy who had done the cane signaling late in the afternoon.

"That fellow Dalny is almost too bad medicine for me to swallow," Dan muttered with a wry smile.

"Of course he is a liar and a villain," Dave returned seriously. "But when a man is wanted to do the foulest kind of work, I suppose it must be rather hard to find a gentleman to volunteer. Probably Dalny's employers feel that they are fortunate enough in being able to obtain the services of a fellow who *looks* like a gentleman."

"He led us into that trap to have us assassinated," Dan declared hotly.

"Or else to have us so badly cut up that we would feel, in the future, more like minding our own business," suggested Ensign Dave with a smile.

"We got out of it all right that time," Dan went on bluntly, "but I don't want any more such experiences. The next time we might not have luck quite so much on our side."

"What puzzles me," Dave continued, wrinkling his brows, "is why Dalny or any of his crowd should want us stabbed."

"They wanted us killed," Dan insisted. "Nothing short of killing us would have satisfied those bravos if they had succeeded in getting us at their mercy. Yet why should our death be desired?''

''For only one reason,'' Dave answered, the truth coming to him in a flash. ''Dalny is here in Naples, for which reason his white-haired fellow-plotter is probably here, too. We were sent ashore to find out if they are here. When Dalny shook hands with us this afternoon he perceived that I recognized him as one whose remarks I undoubtedly had overheard at Monte Carlo. He then concluded that I had been sent ashore to find out if he were here. He knew, or suspected, that I would report my information to the Admiral. Hence the determination to kill me, and, since you are with me, to kill you also. Our bodies would have been hidden, and the Admiral would have been able only to guess why we did not return to the ship. Dan, what hurts me most is the practical certainty that the Count of Surigny is now with that band of international cut-throats. I had hope for a nobler future for the Count, and also I am disappointed to find him working for my enemies. He must hate me fearfully because I thwarted his one-time purpose to commit suicide!''

''I wouldn't have believed the Count could be so bad,'' Dan mused. ''Yet the proof appears to be against him.''

''Why, of course he's one of their band,'' Dave

continued. "It's a fearful thing to say, but it is plain that I saved only an ingrate and a rogue from the crime of suicide. However, Dan, we are losing time. I must begin my report to Captain Allen."

At that instant there came a slight scratching sound at the door. Tiptoeing to the door, Dalzell opened it far enough to admit Seaman Runkle, who, as soon as the door had been closed and locked, promptly saluted both young officers.

"What is your report, Runkle?" Dave demanded.

"Your party in the carriage, sir, dismissed the rig at this address," reported the sailorman, handing Ensign Darrin a slip of paper.

"You did well," Dave answered. "Find a seat, Runkle, until I have written a note which you are to take aboard to Captain Allen."

Within fifteen minutes the letter was completed. It was not a long document, but gave, in brief form, a summary of the adventures and discoveries of the two ensigns since coming ashore.

"You will take this aboard, Runkle," Dave directed, "and you will see that it reaches Captain Allen, even though he has turned in and has to be awakened. You will tell the officer of the deck, with my compliments, that such orders were given me by Captain Allen. Now,

Runkle, don't let anything interfere with your speedy return to the ship. Also remember that you may be followed, and that Naples is a bad town in which to be trailed at night."

"I'm not afraid of the bad people of Naples, sir," rejoined the sailorman, with a quiet smile. "Do you expect me to return to you, sir?"

"That will be as Captain Allen directs."

"Very good, sir. Good night, sir."

Able Seaman Runkle was shown out by Ensign Dalzell, who locked the door of the room after the departing sailorman.

In the meantime a spy who had followed Runkle back to the Hotel dell' Orso had telephoned, in a foreign language little understood in Naples, the information concerning that sailorman's reporting to his officers, and had added the suggestion that very likely the sailor would be sent out to the fleet with a written report.

"I think it highly probable that the sailor *will* be sent with a written report," agreed Mender, at the other end of the telephone wire.

"And if the sailor does try to get out to the fleet?" insinuated the spy.

"If the man leaves the hotel to go to the water front," commanded Mender, in a voice ringing with energy and passion, "see to it that he is laid low and that the letter is taken from him. At any cost I must have turned over to me any written report that Ensign Darrin tries to send to his commanding officer. Nor am I through with Darrin himself!"

CHAPTER XIII

ORDERS CHANGE IN A MINUTE

HULLO! What does that fellow want?"
Able seaman Runkle was within a block
of the mole where the "Hudson's" launch
was due to cast off at half-past ten o'clock, but he
halted in his tracks.

From a doorway, a little nearer to the mole, a
head was thrust out slightly as its owner surveyed
the sailorman.

Then the man stepped out of the doorway to
the sidewalk. He was a big fellow, with something
of the slouch and swagger that are to be observed
in the tough the world over.

Now this stranger stood quite still, sharply
regarding the pausing sailorman.

"If there are less than six of that breed ahead
of me," muttered Runkle, staring ahead once
more, "then it doesn't make any real difference."

Two more men slipped out of dark recesses
further on, while, an instant later, Runkle became aware that two men, who had not been visible

a few moments before, were now closing up behind him.

"I wonder what these chaps think they're going to do," mused Runkle, his sailor heart quaking not at all, though he scented fight in the air. "Hullo!"

Now a sixth man stepped out from a doorway just at his side. With a lusty push this sixth man sent Runkle out into the street.

"Where are your manners, my man?" demanded Seaman Runkle, returning to the sidewalk. "And what do you mean by that?"

Suddenly the muzzle of a revolver gleamed in Runkle's face, but the sailor did not betray any sign of fright.

"Put that down!" ordered Runkle sharply, at the same time making a gesture to indicate his command.

A reply was volubly given in Italian, of which Runkle understood not a word.

In the few seconds that this was happening the five other swarthy men began to close in on the sailor. Runkle lost no time in discovering that fact.

A gesture from the man with the pistol showed that he expected Runkle to hold up his hands.

"You'd rather see my mitts aloft, eh?" asked the sailor, in a mocking voice. "All right, then!"

Up went the sailor's hands, as high as he could raise them. A gleam of satisfaction shone in the eyes behind the revolver, but that look instantly changed to one of pain.

For Runkle, while holding his hands high, also raised one of his feet. That foot went up swiftly, and high enough to land against the lower edge of the bravo's pistol wrist. In a jiffy the wrist was broken and the pistol came clattering to the pavement.

"Much obliged," offered Runkle, snatching up the weapon. Then he raised his voice to yell:

"If there are shipmates within hail let 'em hurry here to keep Jack Runkle from killing a few rattlesnakes!"

Just in time to escape the points of two knives, Seaman Runkle backed against a stucco wall, thrusting out the revolver and his able left fist.

The first two men who leaped at him went down under the impact of that fist. A third received a scalp wound from the butt of the revolver. Any court would have exonerated the sailorman for killing his assailants, but Dave's messenger was much too good-natured to kill while there was another path to safety.

That kindliness undid Runkle's defense. As a man rushed him on each side a third bravo dropped low in front of him and seized the seaman's legs, upsetting him.

"Foul tackle, with a dozen to one!" growled Runkle, as he felt himself going down.

Still he laid about, freeing his feet and using them while he plied his left fist and struck out with the revolver. Even now he did not want to press the trigger of the weapon, which was soon snatched away from him.

With hoarse cries, several of the bravos now held the sailor so that he could barely squirm.

Swiftly moving fingers roamed rapidly through his pockets. Then one of the cowardly assailants snatched out of one of Runkle's pockets a letter, muttering a few words to his companions.

Striking a match the thief glanced at the address on the envelope. Even if he knew no English he could discern that the envelope was addressed to Captain Allen of the "Hudson."

With another quick word the thief vanished through a doorway. Up from the enraged sailor leaped those who had been holding him down.

"Sheer off there! Belay! belay!" growled several hoarse voices. Rushing up, cat-footed, came a dozen or more fresh-faced, husky young jackies from the fleet.

"Come on, mates! The maccaroni-eaters are sneaking away!" yelled the foremost of the rescue party, that had come from the mole in answer to Runkle's call.

Only two of the Italians were slow enough to be overtaken and manhandled by the jackies. The rest of the assailants vanished swiftly into nearby-houses, the doors to which were instantly closed and bolted.

For perhaps twenty seconds the two captured bravos were badly used. Then, thoroughly cowed, they were allowed to slip away.

"What happened to you, shipmate?" demanded one of the rescuers.

"Enough!" growled Runkle. "They got my money."

"Much?"

"All I had."

"Tough luck," declared one of the sailors. "The chap who has your money surely got away before we could reach him."

"I've got to get aboard the flagship as soon as I can," exclaimed Able Seaman Runkle ruefully.

"The launch leaves in ten minutes, mate," volunteered another. "Those of us who are going aboard will now do well to get back to the mole."

So Jack Runkle departed with his rescuers, but his eyes flashed the vengeance he would take should he meet his despoiler again.

On the way out to the flagship Runkle sat silent and out of the run of talk that was going on around him.

Going up over the side of the "Hudson," Runkle reported himself on board, and then added to the officer of the watch, Lieutenant Totten:

"I've a message for the Captain, sir, and have

orders to report to him immediately on coming aboard."

"Orders from an officer of this ship?"

"Yes, sir."

"I'll send an orderly to see if the Captain is still awake," replied Lieutenant Totten.

"I beg your pardon, sir," Runkle persisted, "but I have orders to say that Captain Allen, by his own request, is to be called, if necessary, sir, in order to hear my message."

"Very good," nodded Lieutenant Totten, and turned to an orderly, sending him to Captain Allen's quarters.

"The Captain will see Seaman Runkle at once," the orderly reported a few moments later.

Saluting Lieutenant Totten, Runkle turned and hastily presented himself before the door of the Captain's quarters.

"You have something to report, Runkle?" questioned Captain Allen, seating himself at his desk.

"Yes, sir. Ensign Darrin gave me a letter to bring to you, sir. It may interest you, sir, to know that on my way back to the ship I was attacked near the mole by a mob of cutthroats. One of them held me up with a revolver, but I got it away from him. Then they all attacked me, and soon had me down, sir. One of the rascals took all my money and a letter addressed to you."

"Took Ensign Darrin's letter away from you?" demanded Captain Allen, looking, as he felt, a good deal disturbed.

"No, sir; not Ensign Darrin's letter, sir," replied Able Seaman Runkle, with just a shadow of a grin. "It was a letter addressed to you, but I have reason to believe, sir, that Ensign Darrin's letter is still safe. If you'll permit me, sir, I'll look for the ensign's letter where I placed it, after leaving the ensign and before quitting the hotel."

Captain Allen at once nodded his permission. Runkle partly undressed, then explored the place where he had concealed Dave's letter.

"What was the other letter addressed to me that was taken away from you, Runkle?" questioned the captain, while the search was going on.

"It wasn't really a letter, sir," the sailorman replied, this time with a very broad grin. "It was just an envelope addressed to you, and filled with blank paper."

"Who addressed that envelope?"

"I did, sir."

"And why?"

"Because I thought that Ensign Darrin's letter might be important, and I had an idea that some skulking sneaks might try to take it away from me."

Then Runkle, having put his clothing in order,

stepped towards Captain Allen, holding out an envelope.

"I think, sir, you'll find that this is Ensign Darrin's letter, and that it's just as he gave it to me, sir."

Captain Allen hastily broke the seal, took out the enclosure, and read rapidly, a frown gathering on his face all the while.

"Runkle," cried the Captain, springing up and placing a hand on the sailorman's shoulder, "did Ensign Darrin suggest to you the ruse that fooled your assailants?"

"No, sir."

"You did it on your own initiative?"

"I — I did it out of my own head, sir, if that means the same thing," replied the puzzled sailor slowly.

"It does mean the same thing," continued Captain Allen, "and, Runkle, I'm proud of you. That's a good headpiece you have on your shoulders, and I shall make note of it on your record. You have shown good judgment. You have a head fitted to meet difficulties. You may look for promotion in the near future."

"Have I your permission, sir, to ask if that was Ensign Darrin's letter and if it was in good order?" asked Runkle.

"It was, my man, thanks to your intelligent

and courageous performance of duty. Runkle, how much money did the bravos take from you?"

"Eighteen dollars in real money, sir, and about two dollars in *lira* money."

Sailors sometimes call the Italian money "lira money," because the lire, which is worth about the same as the French *franc*, or twenty cents, is the common unit of Italian currency. "Lira" is the plural of "lire."

"I am afraid you don't like the Italian money very well, Runkle," smiled Captain Allen.

"I don't, sir, and I don't like the people of this country any better. Not after the beating I got to-night."

"That wasn't the fault of the Italian people, Runkle," declared the Captain. "Toughs in New York would use you at least as badly as did the bravos ashore to-night. The Italian people themselves are very friendly to us, and the government does all in its power to show its friendship for our country. If I were to send ashore complaint of your being attacked to-night the police would dragnet the city in an effort to find the men who attacked you, and, if found, it would go hard with them. But for reasons that I cannot explain to you, no complaint will be made. I do not wish the Italian police to know what took place to-night. As to the money that you lost,

I will have you make affidavit before the paymaster, to-morrow, and will see that the money
is repaid to you. Runkle, you may tell your
mates anything you like about the fight, but do
not mention the fact to any one, that you bore
with you and were searched by bravos for a letter
from Ensign Darrin."

"Very good, sir."

"That is all, Runkle. You may go, but remember that I have you in mind as a man of
good and quick judgment, and as one who has
the courage to carry his duty through in the face
of any obstacles."

"Thank you, sir."

Saluting, the sailorman left the Captain's
quarters. A minute later Captain Allen sent
an orderly to the Admiral. Three minutes later
Admiral Timworth received the commanding officer of the flagship.

Quickly Captain Allen placed Dave's letter in
his superior officer's hands.

"This is live news, indeed," cried the Admiral,
as he laid the letter down. "Darrin and Dalzell
are doing clever work."

"But their work is suspected, sir, as the letter
shows. Moreover, the fellow spies of Gortchky
and Dalny are shadowing our two young officers
ashore, for the messenger who brought this letter
was attacked by bravos. Our messenger was

robbed of his money and of a faked letter with which the sailor had provided himself."

Captain Allen then repeated Runkle's story.

"You have Runkle slated for promotion, of course?" asked Admiral Timworth.

"Certainly, sir."

"A man like Runkle, if he keeps to his present promise, should go as high in the Navy as it is possible for an enlisted man to go," declared the Admiral. "But, Captain, the organization and desperation of our country's enemies worry me. It is plain that some very desperate scheme is afoot for making trouble between England and our country. That would drag us in against all of the Entente Allies if the success of the plot should involve us in war with England at this time. The proposed sinking of a British warship is the inkling we have had, but the real scheme may be something else. The first clue of all that we had, even before Darrin and Dalzell came aboard at Gibraltar, came from the American Embassy at Paris. Our Ambassador, under orders from Washington, has our secret service at work there, which keeps our government directly in touch with many of the doings of international plotters. It seems to me highly important that Ensign Darrin should be detached long enough from this ship to be sent to Paris, where he should repeat to our Ambassador all that he knows, and give close descriptions of the spies with whom he has come in contact. Having made his report, Darrin can return to the ship at Genoa, which will be our next port of call in these waters."

"Would you send Mr. Darrin alone, sir?" asked Captain Allen. "He might be trailed and again attacked. Would it not be far better for Ensign Dalzell to go with him?"

"Yes, and perhaps it may be as well for Runkle to go, too, as their orderly," replied the Admiral, after a moment's hesitation. "There is a train leaving for Paris at four in the morning. Where is Lieutenant Totten?"

"He will be off watch in an hour, sir."

"Let Lieutenant Totten go ashore to carry my written instructions to Ensign Darrin. I will enclose the necessary funds in an envelope with my instructions. Totten, on his return to the ship, will be able to assure me that the communication reached Ensign Darrin safely, and that Darrin, after reading my instructions, which will be brief, tore up and burned my letter."

"Shall I send Runkle ashore in uniform or in citizen's dress?" asked Captain Allen.

"In citizen's clothes, as before," replied Admiral Timworth. "I will call my flag lieutenant. Kindly see that the paymaster is sent to me, Captain."

Fifteen minutes later the Admiral's letter of

instruction had been signed, and a substantial amount of money enclosed.

On coming off deck duty at eight bells, midnight, Lieutenant Totten was instructed to order a launch alongside. Then, with the bulky envelope in an inner pocket, and accompanied by Seaman Runkle, Totten went over the side.

A few minutes later the launch delivered them at the mole, then glided out into the bay.

"I hope we shan't run into a gang of hoodlums again," said the sailorman respectfully.

"I have my revolver with me," smiled the lieutenant. "The Italian police would feel grateful if I sank its six bullets into six bravos of Naples."

CHAPTER XIV

DAN HAS VERY "COLD FEET"

RAP-TAP!

That sound brought Dave Darrin out of a sound sleep.   Dan slumbered on.

"Who's there at this hour of the night?" asked Dave, through the door, in the best Italian he could muster.

"From the 'Hudson,'" came the answer, in a voice so low that Dave did not recognize it.

"One minute, then."

Dave slipped back, shaking his chum to rouse him, then drew the curtains around Dalzell's bed.

In record time Dave drew on his own shirt, slipped into trousers, put on collar, cuffs and tie, and followed this with coat and vest.

Then he stepped to the door, opening it.   Repressing his natural cry of astonishment, Dave silently admitted his visitors, next closed and locked the door.

"Orders from the Admiral," said Lieutenant Totten, in an undertone, and passed over the envelope.

Stepping under the light which he had hastily turned on, Darrin read his orders.

"Read this, Dan," said Dave, passing the letter of instructions to his chum, who was now also fully dressed. "Then I will read it once more, after which we will burn it."

"Suits me," commented Dan, when he had finished and was passing back the letter. "I've always wanted to see Paris."

"You won't see much of it this time," smiled Ensign Dave. "This is business, and nothing else."

Then Dave tore the letter into strips. Taking these to the open fireplace he set fire to them. All three officers watched until the letter had been completely burned.

"And now," Dave continued, "I will mix this charred paper thoroughly with the ashes that, fortunately, are left in the grate."

When he had finished, the mixing had been done so well that they would be keen eyes, indeed, that could note the presence of minute particles of burned paper in the grate's contents. His next act was to telephone the hotel clerk to send up a time-table.

"We have plenty of time, yet," smiled Darrin, glancing at his watch, after he had finished consulting the time-table. "It won't be the height of comfort to travel to Paris without baggage.

However, when we get there we can buy anything that we may need."

"It will be great to shop in Paris," cried Dan, his eyes gleaming.

"Don't get the idea that we are going to do any running about in Paris," Dave warned his chum.

"Not even if we have some idle time there?"

"Not even then," Dave answered. "I am very sure that neither the Admiral nor the Ambassador would wish us to show ourselves much at the French capital. We might thereby attract the attention of spies."

"That is true," agreed Lieutenant Totten.

Business being now attended to, Dave and Dan had time to finish dressing comfortably. Then followed a period of waiting. Later the hotel clerk was asked to summon an automobile. In this the Paris-bound party, including Runkle, left the hotel, Totten accompanying them.

No sooner, however, had the American party left the hotel than an Italian, crouching in the shadow of a building further along on the same block, whispered to his companion:

"Telephone Signor Dalny for instructions."

Within three minutes a second automobile rolled up to the hotel.

"To the railway station first, on the chance of finding the Americans there," the spy called to the driver.

Dave's party did not have long to wait at the station. Totten remained with them to the last, however, that he might be able to report a safe start to the Admiral.

"Don't look, sir, but coming up behind you, I am certain, is a fellow I saw on the street outside the hotel just before we started," reported Seaman Runkle.

"Then we are being trailed," Dave said.

Not until the time came for starting did Lieutenant Totten shake hands hurriedly with his brother officers and leave them, though he still stood near the train.

Dave and Dan sprang into their compartment in one of the cars, Able Seaman Runkle following more slowly.

"There's that spy fellow getting on the running-board further down the train, sir," whispered Runkle.

"I expected him," answered Dave dryly.

"Would you like to lose him, sir?"

"Off the train altogether, do you mean, Runkle?"

"Yes, sir."

"Can you put him off without hurting him?"

"I think I can get him off, sir, without even scraping one of his knuckles."

"You're at liberty to try, Runkle, if you are sure you won't injure the man."

As the guard came along, locking the doors, Runkle leaped down to the ground.

"Help, Mr. Totten, help!" called the seaman in a low voice that none the less reached the ears of the departing lieutenant.

Then Runkle moved directly up to the spy leering into his face and making insulting signs that caused the fellow to flush red.

"You're no good — savvy?" insisted Runkle in a low tone, making more faces and gestures.

So quickly was it done that the now thoroughly insulted spy, though he did not understand English, leaped at Runkle in a rage.

"He's going to try to rob me, sir!" cried Runkle, not very effectively dodging the blows that the fellow aimed at him.

"Here, what are you up to?" demanded Totten, also in English, as he reached out to grab the spy's collar.

In that strong grip the spy writhed, but could not escape.

"Thank you, sir," cried Runkle, with an unmistakable wink, after which he raced for the car and the compartment in which the two young ensigns waited.

"Lieutenant Totten is holding on to the chap, sir," announced Runkle gleefully. "He won't let him go until the train's out, either."

Holding the unlocked door open a crack, Dan

Dalzell watched as the train pulled away from the station.

"Totten has him, and is explaining to a policeman," Dalzell chuckled. "That spy doesn't travel with us this trip."

"What's the odds?" asked Darrin, after a pause. "Dalny must belong to a big and clever organization. He can wire ahead to spies who will board the train later on and follow us into Paris."

"Then, with your leave, sir, I'll keep my eye open for spies until we're back aboard the flagship," suggested Runkle.

"Very good, so long as you break neither laws nor bones, Runkle," Dave laughed.

The Americans had the compartment to themselves. Had all been in uniform Runkle would not have been likely to travel in the same compartment with the young officers, but in citizen's dress much of discipline could be waived for greater safety.

Though Dan Dalzell did not now have much hope of sightseeing in Paris, he was able, after dozing until daylight, to gaze interestedly out upon the country through which he was traveling.

Able Seaman Runkle was another absorbed window-gazer. As for Ensign Dave Darrin, while he caught many interesting glimpses of the scenery, his mind was mainly on the question of how the international plotters were planning to break the friendship between the two strongest nations on earth.

By what means could these plotters sink a British ship, and yet make it appear to be the work of Americans?

Hundreds of miles had been traveled, and one day had swung far on into another before a plausible answer came to Darrin's mind.

Then Dave fairly jumped — the thing that Admiral Timworth so dreaded now looked quite easy.

"What's the matter?" asked Dan, staring at his chum.

"Why?" countered Dave.

"You jumped so hard," Dan replied.

"I was thinking."

"Stop it!" advised Danny Grin. "A little harder thinking than that might wreck the train."

Dalzell enjoyed every hour of the journey. In the daylight hours he was busy "taking in" all the country through which the train passed. In the evening hours, Dan was outside on the platform, at every station, to watch the crowds, large or small.

As for Seaman Runkle, that splendid lad was absorbed, almost to the point of gloom, in watching at every station for a sign of a spy on the train with them.

Before they reached the French-Italian frontier Dave realized, with a start, that Admiral Timworth had failed to provide them with such credentials as would probably be called for in crossing the Italian-French frontier, and that they had forgotten to ask for such papers. However, at the frontier stop their friend Dandelli, the Italian naval officer, in uniform, almost ran into them. He was glad to vouch for the pair to the French and Italian guards at that point, and, after some hesitation, Dave and Dan were allowed to proceed into France.

"But be careful to have proper papers when returning, if you come this way," Dandelli smilingly warned them.

It was seven o'clock on the second morning after leaving Naples when the express reached Paris.

Hardly had the train stopped when Darrin and Dalzell were out and moving through the station. Seaman Runkle kept at a distance behind them, his sharp eyes searching for any signs of spies. But Runkle was able to make no report of success when he stepped into the taxicab in which his superior officers sat.

Danny Grin was again busy with his eyes as the taxicab darted through the beautiful streets of the French capital.

"What are you laughing at?" Dave asked suddenly, noting that Dan's grin was even wider than usual.

"Paris strikes me that way — that's all I can tell you," drawled Dan.

"Do you consider Paris a joke?" demanded Darrin.

"Of course not. But Paris has the name of being such a gay town — in peace times, of course. But at this early hour the city looks actually gray to me. If the look of the city doesn't improve, later in the day, I can't understand how any one can feel like being gay."

"Paris and the world have managed well enough, in the past, to combine for gayety," Dave replied. "Just now, of course, with all the men thinking of war, and so many women wearing black for dear ones they've lost at the front, the city can't show much of its former gayety. Paris is going through her ordeal of fire. These are dark days for good old France!"

Suddenly Dan's face fell grave.

"Now, what's the matter?" quizzed Darrin.

"I've just had a horrible thought," Dan confessed. "You haven't been concealing from me, have you, the fact that, though you had no frontier passport you have a letter or some form of credentials to the American Ambassador?"

"I haven't anything of the sort," Dave rejoined, he, too, now looking grave.

"A fine lay-out this is, then," growled Danny Grin. "Here we are, going to the American

Ambassador on a matter of the utmost delicacy. We are going to tell him and ask him some of the secrets of the United States government, and we haven't a scrap of paper to introduce us. Do you realize what we'll get? The Johnny-run-quick! We'll get the balluster slide, the ice-pitcher greeting! Dave, we're going to land hard on the sidewalk right in front of the Embassy. And then some frog-eating, Johnny Crapaud policeman will gather us in as disorderly persons! Fine!"

CHAPTER XV

AT THE AMERICAN EMBASSY

A S the taxicab dashed around a corner Dave raised his cap.

"Well, this must be our destination," he announced. "I've just saluted Old Glory as it flutters over the building."

The taxicab came to a stop before a handsome building.

On each side of the posts of the gateway stood a brass shield on which was the inscription:

"Embassy of the United States of America."

Very gravely Dan and Runkle followed Dave, each raising his hat to the Flag as soon as his feet touched the sidewalk.

"There's a carriage entrance below," said Dave, "but we'll take the plain way and walk in."

Paying and dismissing the taxicab driver, Dave led the way to the entrance.

"A naval party to see the Ambassador, at his convenience, on business," Dave announced to the attendant at the door.

They were shown to an anteroom near the

door, where they were soon joined by a Mr. Lupton, who introduced himself as Second Secretary to the Embassy.

"The ambassador, Mr. Caine, will not be here before nine o'clock," announced Mr. Lupton. "I know that you are expected. You have not breakfasted?"

"No," Dave confessed.

"Then I will ask you to let me be host. Before I lead the way I will ring for some one to see that your sailorman is well taken care of."

Five minutes later Darrin and Dalzell were seated at a small breakfast table with Mr. Lupton.

"Just before reaching here," began Dave, "it occurred to Mr. Dalzell and myself that we have, beyond our card-cases, no means of identification. Can you tell us how Mr. Caine will be sure that he is talking with the right persons?"

"I believe that will be arranged all right," smiled Mr. Lupton. "I, too, have taken you gentlemen on trust, but presently, I believe, we are going to be satisfied."

Two minutes later there stalked into the room a tall, handsome young man whose navy uniform set off his good figure to great advantage.

"Jetson?" exclaimed Dave, rising.

"The same," smiled the new-comer, advancing and holding out his hand.

He and Dave shook hands heartily, after which
Dan came in for a similar greeting.

Readers of the Annapolis series will recall
Jetson as being a fellow member of the Brigade
of Midshipmen with Darrin and Dalzell at the
U. S. Naval Academy. At one time, there,
Dave and Jetson had not been good friends, but
Dave had, at the very great risk of his own life,
saved Jetson from drowning. Now, the two young
officers were on excellent terms.

"I understand, now, what was darkness to
me before," murmured Dave, after Jetson had
seated himself at table. "Admiral Timworth
knew that you were here, Jetson, and able to
identify us."

"I have been here for three months," explained
Jetson, smiling, "doing some work to assist the
naval attaché of this Embassy, Commander
Tupper. I have had three months of the hardest
work in this old capital, but now, confound it,
my work here has ended and I'm ordered to join
my ship. The bridge and the quarter-deck are
places of boredom to a fellow who has seen what
I've seen here. Why, I've even made two trips
up to the front — one of them to Verdun."

"Lucky dog!" cried Danny Grin, with feeling.
"So you've seen some of the big fighting!"

"It may be well to state that I know fully the
business on which you are ordered here," Jetson

continued, "so you may mention it freely before me if you are so inclined."

"Then can you tell me," Dave asked, "if it is known how our enemies propose to sink a British warship and make it appear to be the work of someone in the American Navy?"

"I cannot," Jetson replied. "In fact, it was only on receipt of a wireless from near Monte Carlo that the Ambassador had any knowledge that the international plotters intended to attempt the destruction of a British warship as a means for creating bad feeling between the two countries. The whole plot seems foolishly improbable to me."

"It doesn't seem so to me, any longer," rejoined Dave.

"Then you must know some thing that I haven't heard about," murmured Jetson curiously.

"Mr. Darrin," broke in Mr. Lupton, "I will be the Ambassador's authority for you to speak as freely of the matter as you choose."

Dave and Dan thereupon told all that had befallen them at Monte Carlo and at Naples.

"But still," Jetson broke in perplexedly, "how is the sinking of a British warship to be brought about with safety to the plotters, and how is the crime to be laid at the door of the American Navy?"

"I wish to speak to the Ambassador on that point before I mention it to any one else," Dave answered.

"Have you told Dalzell?" pressed Jetson.

"I have not."

"He certainly hasn't," complained Danny Grin sadly. "Dave always tells me after he has told every one else."

"Danny boy," Dave rebuked him, "where do you hope to go after you die?"

"Paris," Dalzell answered promptly.

Breakfast lasted until word came that the Ambassador was ready to receive the two young officers from the flagship of the Mediterranean Fleet. Then Jetson left his friends.

Mr. Caine, to whom Mr. Lupton presently introduced the ensigns, was a man in his fifties, rather bald, and with a decided stoop in his shoulders. At home he was a manufacturer of barbed wire, and his business, as Danny later suggested, had perhaps helped to give him some of his keenness and sharpness. He was slenderly fashioned, and reminded one, at first, of a professor in a minor college.

It was when the Ambassador transacted business that some of his sterling qualities came out. He was recognized as being one of the cleverest and ablest of American diplomats.

"I am glad to meet you, gentlemen," said the

Ambassador, shaking hands with Dave and Dan
and then motioning them to seats, which an
attendant placed for them. "Mr. Lupton, you
have doubtless had Jetson's assurance that these
young men are the persons they claim to be?"

"Yes, sir," Lupton rejoined.

"Then tell me all you can of this matter,"
urged Mr. Caine.

At a look from Second Secretary Lupton, the
attendant withdrew from the room. Dave and
Dan were soon deep in the narration of events
in which they participated at Monte Carlo and
at Naples.

"I know the young Comte of Surigny," remarked Mr. Caine, "and I am deeply disappointed
to learn that he is among our foes, and in such a
mean capacity as the one in which he must be
employed. The young man comes from one of
the most ancient families in France, though he
has never been well-to-do, for his ancestors attended to the insuring of his poverty. The gambling streak has run through several generations
of the family."

Then Dave and Dan continued with their
story, Ambassador Caine paying close attention
to all they said.

"Gortchky is expected in Paris soon," announced the Ambassador presently.

"Is he, sir?" Darrin asked quickly. "Would

it be indiscreet for me to ask if you know why he
is coming here?"

"I have nothing more definite than suspicion,"
replied Mr. Caine. "Paris, which has one of the
best detective systems of the world, is also noted
as being the principal headquarters for con-
spiracies against governments. Not only do the
anarchists and nihilists look upon Paris as their
Mecca; but other scoundrels working out nefarious
plans for wicked governments also meet here to
lay their dastardly plots. Gortchky may be
coming here to secure new agents to take the
place of those already known to the Americans
who are watching him and his men; or he may
be coming here to hold a conference with the
men higher up, who are directing his scoundrelly
work against the peace of England and America."

"I take it, sir, that your secret service men will
make every effort to find out what Gortchky does
in Paris, and for what real purpose he is here,
and —"

Here Ensign Dave Darrin broke off abruptly,
coloring deeply.

"I beg your pardon, sir," he apologized hurriedly. "I had no right to ask you such ·a
question."

"I have no objection to answering you," said
the Ambassador seriously. "Of course my men
will make every effort to find out what Gortchky

is up to here, if he comes to Paris, but I do not know how well they will succeed. In the game of making trouble between nations Emil Gortchky is an old and wary bird. It may very likely be that the fellow is coming to Paris only to try to draw my secret service men into the worst kind of a wild-goose chase leading only to clues that are worse than worthless. Gortchky, in other words, may be on his way to Paris only to draw our attention away from vital moves about to be made elsewhere by other members of his rascally band. Of course, on due complaint, we could have him arrested as a spy, and it would go hard with him here in Paris before a military court. But in that case there are others in the band of plotters whom we do not know and cannot locate. So, for very good reasons, we prefer to have Gortchky at large."

"I would like immensely to see Gortchky in Paris," Dave muttered.

"Perhaps you will have your wish," replied Mr. Caine, with an odd smile.

Soon after that the interview came to an end, but Dave and Dan remained in the Embassy building through the day. An attendant was sent out to get them what they needed in linen and other small items.

Dinner was to be served at seven o'clock, and, as Mr. Caine did not wish the presence of the young officers from the Mediterranean Fleet in his house to be known, it was arranged that they should dine in a smaller room alone with Mr. Lupton.

At six, however, the Ambassador sent in haste for Dave to come to his office.

"That invitation doesn't seem to include me," remarked Dalzell, rather ruefully, as he glanced up from a book he was reading in the Embassy library.

"I'm afraid it doesn't," Dave returned.

Mr. Caine was at his office desk, holding a telegram sheet in his hand.

"Gortchky is expected in town at 7.30 this evening, Mr. Darrin," announced the Ambassador.

"Is there anything that I can do in this matter, sir?" Darrin asked, after a pause.

"You may go and watch for Gortchky, if you think it possible to do so without his detecting you," Mr. Caine replied slowly.

"The opportunity would delight me beyond measure," Dave rejoined quickly. "I suppose I had better take a taxicab that I may be ready to give effective chase in case Emil Gortchky uses that kind of transportation."

"I can supply you with a taxicab and with a chauffeur who can be trusted," replied the Ambassador. "The driver I have in mind is a highly intelligent fellow who has many times been employed by me. And you can dismiss him at any point, or retain him as long as you wish. The bill for the taxicab charges will be sent to the Embassy. How soon do you wish to have this taxicab here?"

"Perhaps I should have it at once," Dave replied. "Gortchky would know me in these clothes at first glance, so it would be advantageous if I arranged to disguise myself. On the streets, as we came here, I noticed not a few young men wearing baggy suits of clothes of most un-American cut. They wore also flowing neckties, and some of them had blue eyeglasses. There are so many of these young men about that one more would hardly attract Gortchky's attention. That style of dress would make a good disguise for me."

"The young men you describe are largely students and artists," replied the Ambassador. "A disguise of that kind would be less conspicuous than any other."

"Then, sir, if the chauffeur can come here soon, he will have time to take me to stores where I can get the articles of apparel I need, and I shall still have plenty of time to meet Emil Gortchky if he reaches Paris this evening. I will go and tell Mr. Dalzell about Gortchky being expected to arrive here to-night."

"Tell Mr. Dalzell if you wish, but you had better not take him with you," replied Mr.

Caine. "Two young men would attract more attention than one. I am approving of your undertaking this because, to date, you have learned more about this conspiracy than any three of the secret service men whom I have at my orders."

Dave hurried away to Dan, who was highly disappointed at being left out of the evening's work.

"But I have the joke on you, anyway," Danny Grin suddenly declared.

"How so?" asked Dave.

"I shall have my dinner," laughed Dalzell; "you won't have any."

"I could forget my meals for three whole days to stay on the trail of Gortchky," Dave answered, simply.

Then he hurried out, for the arrival of the taxicab was now announced. Darrin had a minute's conversation with the chauffeur, after which he entered the car.

One thing the young ensign quickly discovered, and that was that on the smooth pavements of Paris, and in the well-ordered traffic, taxicabs travel at a high rate of speed. Within five minutes he had been set down at the door of a shop in which he found it possible to buy every item of his disguise, even to shoes, for Darrin suddenly remembered that his footwear was plainly American.

In fifteen minutes more Dave Darrin emerged from the store. In one hand he carried his discarded clothing, packed in a new bag, which he turned over to the chauffeur for safe keeping. All of his money, except a small sum, he had left behind at the Embassy.

If any policeman had seen him enter the shop and come out again presenting so changed an appearance, and if for that reason the policeman should question him under the impression that Darrin might be a spy, Dave decided that he would rely upon his chauffeur to declare that he had been hired at the American Embassy. That statement would remove suspicion.

"You had better kill time for a few minutes," Dave explained to the chauffeur, who understood English. "It is not desirable to reach the railway station earlier than 7.20."

Accordingly the young ensign enjoyed a brief, rapid panoramic view of a considerable part of Paris. The driver, accustomed to taking Americans about who were strangers in the city, frequently turned his head to offer information as to the places or points of interest that they were passing.

"It's a shame that Danny boy isn't here to enjoy all this," Dave told himself. "Even this way of seeing Paris would be a great treat to him."

Almost to the second of 7.20 the taxicab drew up as one of a long line of similar vehicles under the bright lights of the railway station.

Alighting, Ensign Darrin, feeling rather well concealed in his disguise, and looking out through his blue-lensed eyeglasses, strolled about, careful not to saunter into the most brilliantly lighted spots.

Presently he heard a train enter the station. A thin stream of passengers filtered out. Dave promptly shifted his position and watched the arrivals, who later came out in a more compact throng.

And there was Emil Gortchky, at last, with no more marked hand luggage than a light cane, which he swung jauntily.

"I hope you don't look my way, my fine bird!" uttered Ensign Darrin under his breath. "But if you do, your observation won't do you much good."

A hand beckoned from a taxicab. Emil Gortchky, who had been on the lookout, sauntered over to the vehicle and clasped the hand of M. le Comte de Surigny.

"Surigny, the ungrateful!" uttered Dave disgustedly to himself. "I induced you to spare your own worthless life, and then when you found life sweet once more, you turned against me! I hope you did not notice me as you sat in that cab."

By this time Dave was at the side step of his own taxicab. A few words to the chauffeur, and he entered.

Surigny's cab drew out of the line, gliding away. The one in which Dave sat gave chase at a cautious distance.

Soon the speed of the leading cab increased, and the pursuing one followed at the same speed. After a considerable run both cabs turned into the broad, well-lighted Boulevard Haussman. For some blocks both cabs ran along. Then the one ahead turned in before an imposing-looking building with a gleaming white marble front.

"The Grand Prix Club," explained Dave's chauffeur, glancing back as he stopped on the other side of the boulevard some distance to the rear.

It was the Count of Surigny who left the cab, which then started forward.

"Is there gambling going on in that club?" asked Darrin, as his man started the car forward again.

"Naturally," replied the chauffeur, shrugging his shoulders.

"It is easy to understand, then," Dave muttered to himself. "Poor Surigny is no longer his own master in anything, for he is a slave to the gambling craze that ruins so many lives. Gortchky furnishes the young man with money for gambling — lends it to him, of course, and thus keeps the Count desperately in his debt. And so the young Count has to do, when required, the bidding of the scoundrel who gloats over the helplessness of his dupe. Poor Surigny!"

Into less handsome avenues and streets the taxicabs now turned. Then a distinctly shabby looking part of Paris was unfolded to the gaze of the young naval officer.

"The Rue d'Ansin," announced the chauffeur, at last.

"A bad street?" Dave inquired.

"Yes."

"The haunt of criminals?"

"Criminals are seen here," the chauffeur explained, "but their real lurking places are in some of the alleys, farther along, that lead off from the Rue d'Ansin. Late at night, monsieur, it is better to ride through this street than to be afoot on the sidewalk!"

"Is it the part of Paris where one would come to meet or to confer with desperate criminals?" Dave asked.

"Many of the Apaches live hereabouts," replied the chauffeur, with another shrug.

Dave had read of these dangerous thugs, the so-called "Apaches," native toughs of Paris, who commit many bold robberies on the streets by night, and even, sometimes, by day, and

who seldom hesitate to kill a victim or a policeman if murder will render their own escape sure.

To an observer the Apache appears to be equally
without fear and without conscience. The Apache
is many degrees more dangerous than his more
cowardly cousin, the "gun-man" of New York.

"I hope you will not have to take to the streets
here, Monsieur," said the chauffeur.

"If I have to do that, I am not afraid to take
a chance," Darrin answered, imitating the Frenchman's shrug with his own broad shoulders.

Ahead, Gortchky's taxicab was slowing down,
and the pursuing vehicle did the same. Dave
peered about to see if some one were waiting to
be taken up by Gortchky, but, instead, Gortchky
descended.

"Drive close to the curb on the other side of
the street," whispered Darrin. "Merely slow
down so that I may slip to the sidewalk. Then
go ahead, waiting for me around the corner two
blocks away."

"One block away would be better, Monsieur,"
urged the chauffeur.

"Make it two," Dave insisted crisply.

Stepping out on the running board, Dave
leaned well forward, thus making it possible to
close the door of his car as it slowed down. Then,
as Dave stepped to the sidewalk, the taxicab
moved forward more rapidly.

Searching in an inner pocket, Emil Gortchky, down the street on the other side, did not look up, and apparently did not observe the maneuver on the part of Dave's chauffeur. Dave slipped quickly into a darkened doorway, from which he could watch the international spy with little danger of being observed.

Taking out a little packet of papers, and moving toward a street lamp, Gortchky selected one of the papers, thrusting the rest back into his pocket. As he did so, one white bit fluttered to the sidewalk.

Reading under the street lamp the paper he had selected, Gortchky put that particular paper in another pocket. Then he turned abruptly, plunging into the depths of an alley-like street.

Sauntering slowly across the street, in order not to attract too much attention from other passers on the badly lighted Rue d'Ansin, Ensign Darrin, his gaze glued to that piece of paper, soon reached it and picked it up.

"For that scoundrel to drop this paper, of all others that he had in his pocket!" gasped Dave Darrin, as, under the street light, he took in its nature.

Then he paled, for this paper seemed to confirm absolutely the young ensign's suspicion as to the way in which the British battleship was to be destroyed.

All in a twinkling Dave's pallor vanished, for he had something else to think about.

On the alley-like side street a quick step was heard that Darrin recognized. It was that of Emil Gortchky, hastily returning to find the paper that he had dropped in the heart of Apache Land!

CHAPTER XVI

"SEEING" THE PARIS APACHES

L IKE a flash Darrin thrust the paper into one of his own pockets. Then he turned, darting into a near-by doorway dark enough to conceal him from Gortchky's eyes, if he should look in that direction.

"I've no reason for fearing an encounter with Gortchky, unless he knows how to summon the murderous Apaches to his aid," Dave told himself as he pressed back as far as he could into his hiding place. "I don't want Gortchky, however, to know I'm watching him, and I don't want to lose this precious paper any more than he does."

Touching the door accidentally with the hand that rested behind his back, Dave was delighted to feel it swing slightly open. In another instant he had backed into a corridor, softly closing the door after him.

"Now Gortchky won't find me, and I'm all right, unless I am discovered by one of the occupants of this house, and turned over to the police as a burglar!" thought the young naval officer exultantly.

Gortchky's step, now slower, went by the door, which Dave had left ajar by only the tiniest crack.

"I cannot have lost that paper here, after all," Dave heard the international spy mutter in a low voice. "Certainly it has not been picked up, for I came back almost instantly, and there was no one near. It is not likely that I shall ever see that important little bit of paper again."

Yet for a few moments longer Dave heard the international spy moving about as though still searching. Then the fellow's footsteps died out as he went around the corner.

"I'll wait a few minutes before I step out," Darrin decided. "Gortchky may only be laying a trap, and even at this instant he may be peering around the corner to see if any one steps out of one of these doorways."

Waiting for what seemed to be a long time, but what was actually only a few minutes, the young ensign stepped out to the sidewalk again.

There were a few people on his own side of the block, and the sight of any one leaving a house was not likely to arouse curiosity in the minds of the denizens of that neighborhood.

As Dave neared the next corner, however, four rough-looking fellows came out of a little café. Their bearing was full of swagger. These young men, in dress half student and half laborer, with caps pulled down over their eyes and gaily-knotted handkerchiefs around their necks, displayed the shifting, cunning look that is found in the hoodlum everywhere.

As they reached the sidewalk, moving with the noiseless step peculiar to the Apache, they heard Darrin briskly coming along. Halting, they regarded him closely as he neared them.

"They look like hard characters," Dave told himself. "However, if I mind my business, I guess they'll mind theirs."

It was not to be. One of the Apaches, the tallest and slimmest of the lot, regarded Darrin with more curiosity than did any of the others.

"Ho!" he cried. "See how stiffly our little student carries himself! He must have been to see his sweetheart, and feels proud of himself."

"He has the stride of a banker," jeered another. "I wonder if he has his bank with him."

Dave's ear, quickly attuned to the French tongue, caught and understood the words.

"Let me see what you look like," urged the slim fellow, reaching out and plucking from Darrin's nose the blue eye glasses just as Dave was passing the group.

That gesture and the act were so insulting that Ensign Darrin could not keep back the flash that leaped into his eyes. He halted, regarding the Apache steadily.

"Why, bless me! He's an American!" cried
the Apache. "All Americans are rich, you know.
My friend, have you a few sous for a group of
poor workingmen?"

Dave essayed to pass on. As he did so, a foot
was thrust out. Dave saw the movement and
leaped over the foot to avoid being tripped.

"At him!" hissed the slim Apache. "Let us
shake out his pockets."

Dave sprang forward, although he knew that
he could not hope to run away. Instead, he
leaped to a wall, placing his back against it. There
he halted, glaring defiantly at his assailants, his
fists up and ready for instant action.

"Sail in! Trim him!" snarled the slim one.
"If our little American shows fight — kill him!"

The first who reached Dave reeled back with
a broken nose, for Darrin's first was hard.

"Stick the pig!" cried the leader, meaning
that the young officer was to be stabbed. Not
one of the four had a knife, it seemed.

As they surrounded him, the one with the
injured nose having returned to the fray, that
slim Apache drew out a sandbag, long and narrow, shaped like a sausage, made of canvas
and filled with sand. This is one of the most
deadly weapons in the world.

"Let us see what soothing medicine will do!"
he jeered.

In an instant all four had brought sandbags to light, and all closed in upon the desperate American.

"Come on, you cowards!" roared Dave, forgetting his French and lapsing back into English. "If I go out I'll take one of you with me."

Trying to tantalize their victim, the Apaches made thrusts at Ensign Dave, and then leaped nimbly back. It was their hope that he would spring forward at them and thus leave his rear unguarded. It is easiest to use the sandbag on a victim from behind, though the tactics now employed were favorites with the Apaches.

Dave had sense enough to divine the nature of their trick. Unless the police arrived promptly he expected to be killed by these jeering scoundrels, but he was determined to sell his life dearly enough.

Suddenly the young naval officer saw his chance and used it. One of his dancing tormentors got in too close. Darrin's right foot shot up and out, landing across the Apache's knee-cap.

Uttering a howl of rage and pain, the fellow all but crawled back.

"Kill the American," he howled. "Don't play with him."

Instantly the three remaining assailants worked in closer, yet with all the caution of their wily natures.

"Rush me!" taunted Dave, again in English. "Don't be so afraid. If you mean to kill me why don't you show courage enough to do it? Come on, you sneaks!"

Though the Apaches could not understand what the young ensign said to them, they knew the drift of his jeering words. Their faces contorted with rage, they struck at him, Dave's arms working like piston rods in his efforts to ward off their blows.

Close to the wall, slipping along on tip-toe came a tall figure. Then suddenly a newcomer leaped into the picture.

Biff! smash! Struck from behind in the neck, two of the Apaches pitched forward, going to earth. Dave Darrin, with a feint, followed up with a swinging right-hand uppercut, laid the last of the Apaches low, for the fellow sitting in a doorway, nursing his knee and cursing, no longer counted.

"Quick! Out of here!" ordered the newcomer, seizing Dave by the arm and starting him along.

"Jetson!" gasped Ensign Darrin, looking into the face of his rescuer.

"Yes," answered his brother officer. "Hurry along!"

"Jetson, you've saved my life this time. That pack of wolves would have killed me in spite of my best defense."

"We're not out of trouble yet," retorted Jetson, fairly pushing Darrin along. "Those Apaches will revive in a few seconds."

"Pooh! Together, Jetson, we could thrash half a dozen of their kind, and find it only exercise."

"But, my boy, don't you realize that there are more than three or four Apaches around the Rue d'Ansin? The alarm will sound, and a score more will rush up. These rascals are sure death, Darry, if they get at you in sufficient numbers! The Parisians fear them. You don't see a single citizen on the street now. Look! Every one of them flew to cover as soon as the Apaches moved into action. If bystanders interfered, or even watched, they too would have to reckon with these Apaches. Now, Darry, you're no coward, and neither am I, but if you're wise you will imitate me by taking to your heels."

Still holding Dave's arm lightly, Jetson sprinted along to the next corner.

"To the right," whispered Dave. "I've a taxicab here."

More than halfway down the block they saw the car at the curb. The chauffeur, when Dave called, stepped from a doorway in which he had taken refuge.

"The Apaches!" gasped the driver.

"Hustle!" urged Dave. "Come on, Jetson."

As the two young naval officers sprang into the car, the driver leaped to his own seat. Pressing the self-starter, the chauffeur soon had his machine gliding along. Nor did he go back, either, by way of the Rue d'Ansin.

Not until he was four blocks away from the scene did the man ask for his orders.

"Back to the Embassy," Dave instructed him. Then he remembered his comrade's swift, fine rescue.

"Jetson," he asked, "did you know it was I who was menaced by the Apaches?"

"I did not," replied his brother officer. "But I heard enough, at a distance, to know that an American was in trouble. In Paris that is sufficient for me. Darry, I am delighted that I happened along in time."

"You saved my life, Jetson, and at the risk of your own. If you had missed one of the Apaches, or had lost your balance, your career would have been ended right there, along with mine."

"You risked your life for me, Darry, back in the old Annapolis days, so we are even," answered Jetson gently. "However, we won't keep books on the subject of brotherly aid. All I can say, Darry, is that I am glad I chose this night to call on an artist who lives in dingy quarters half a mile beyond where I found you. And I am also glad that I did not accept his invitation

to supper, or I should have come along too late
to serve you."

As soon as the machine had left them at the
Embassy, Darrin sought out Mr. Lupton.

"May I see Mr. Caine at once?" asked the
young officer.

"You have seen Gortchky, then?"

"Yes, and I have found what I consider
positive proof as to the plans of Gortchky's
crew."

"I think Mr. Caine can be seen," replied
Lupton.

Ensign Darrin was soon with the American
Ambassador, who nodded to Lupton to leave
the room.

"Here, sir," began Darrin, "is a bit of
paper that Gortchky dropped and which I
picked up."

Mr. Caine scanned the paper.

"I do not see anything so very remarkable
about it," he replied.

Dave whispered a few words in his ear

"Is that true?" asked the Ambassador, dis-
playing sudden agitation.

"Yes, sir."

"Then I believe you are right, Darrin,"
gasped the Ambassador, sinking back into
his chair, his face paling slightly. "Oh the
villains!"

"Then you believe, sir, that I have really discovered the plot?" asked Dave, who looked only a whit less agitated.

"If what you have just told me is true, then it must be that you have made a correct guess."

"Will you send word by wireless to Admiral Timworth, then, sir?"

"I dare not trust such news, even to the cipher, which the international gang thought they had filched, and which they did not get," replied Mr. Caine. "I believe that the wisest course will be for you to take the midnight train to Genoa."

"Then I shall take this paper with me?"

"Yes, Mr. Darrin, for the Admiral is far more capable than I of estimating it at its true worth. It is a matter for a naval man to comprehend and decide."

The Ambassador did not neglect to provide the young ensign with documents, approved by the French Foreign Office, that would take them safely over the border into Italy on their return trip.

CHAPTER XVII

DAVE'S GUESS AT THE BIG PLOT

"FRIENDS tell me that in being in the Navy I have such a grand chance to see the world," grumbled Dan Dalzell, as the launch headed for the anchorage of the American warships. "I went to Paris and had two short taxicab rides through the city. That was all I saw of Paris. Then a long railway journey, and I reached Genoa. I spent twenty-eight minutes in Genoa, and boarded this launch. Oh, I'm seeing the world at a great rate! By the time I'm an admiral I shall know nearly as much of the world as I did when I studied geography in the Central Grammar School of Gridley."

"Don't be a kicker, Danny boy," smiled Dave. "And just think! When you get home, if any one asks you if you've been in Paris, you can say 'Yes.' Should any one ask you if you've seen Genoa, you can hold up your head and declare that you have."

"But my friends will ask me to tell them about those towns," complained Dalzell.

"Read them up in the guide books," advised

Jetson, who was of the party. "I've known a lot of Navy officers who got their knowledge of foreign places in that way."

Dave and Dan had had but a fleeting glimpse of the fine city that now lay astern of them. Hundreds of sailormen and scores of officers, on sight-seeing bent, had been ashore for two days.

But now the recall to the fleet had come. All save Darrin, Dalzell and Jetson, with Seaman Runkle, who was now up forward on the launch, were already aboard their respective ships. The Admiral waited only for the coming of this launch before he gave the sailing order.

Jetson was assigned to the battleship "Allegheny," a craft only a trifle smaller than the massive "Hudson."

The three brother officers and Runkle had traveled by express from Paris to Genoa, and had come through without incident. At last even the watchful Runkle was convinced that they had eluded all spies.

"Boatswain's Mate," said Dave, "as this launch belongs to the flagship, it will be better to take Mr. Jetson, first, over to his ship."

"Aye, aye, sir," responded the man in charge of the launch.

Twenty minutes later Dave Darrin found himself leading his own party up over the side of the "Hudson."

"Captain Allen wishes to see Ensigns Darrin and Dalzell at once," announced Lieutenant Cranston, the officer of the deck. "You will report to the Captain without further instructions."

"Very good, sir," Dave answered, saluting.

Exactly ten minutes later the two young ensigns were ushered into the presence of their commanding officer.

"Admiral Timworth has been notified by wireless from Paris that you have important communications to make to him," began the Captain. "I will not waste your time or the Admiral's in questioning you here. You will come with me to the fleet commander's quarters. The Admiral is awaiting you."

Admiral Thomas Timworth, seated at his desk, and with his flag lieutenant standing by, greeted his callers with exceeding briskness.

"Gentlemen," he said, "time presses, and we must dispense with formalities. Ensign Darrin, I am advised by the Ambassador at Paris of the importance of your news, but he does not tell me what the news is."

"Its importance, sir, depends on whether the evidence I have to present supports the guess I have made as to the nature of the plot that has been planned against the peace and safety of Great Britain and our own country."

As Dave spoke he produced from an inner pocket the sheet of paper dropped by Gortchky, that he had picked up in the Rue d'Ansin.

"This piece of paper, sir," Darrin continued, passing it to the fleet commander, "is one that I *saw* Emil Gortchky drop from a packet of several papers that he took from his pocket at night on one of the worst streets in the slums of Paris."

Admiral Timworth scanned the paper, then read it aloud. It was a receipted bill, made out in the name of one unknown to those present, though perhaps an alias for Gortchky himself. The bill was for a shipment of storage batteries. At the bottom of the sheet was a filled-in certificate signed by a French government official, to the effect that the batteries had been shipped into Italy "for laboratory purposes of scientific research." Just below this statement was an official Italian certificate of approval, showing that the batteries had been admitted into Italy. In time of war, with the frontier guarded tenfold more vigilant than in ordinary times, such certificates are vitally necessary to make shipments from France into Italy possible.

"In other words, sir," Dave went on eagerly, when the fleet commander scanned his face closely, "it needed some very clever underhand work, very plausibly managed, to make it possible to buy those batteries in France and to secure their admittance into Italy."

"Why?" quizzed Admiral Timworth, as though he did not know the answer himself.

"Because, sir," Dave went on keenly, full of professional knowledge of the subject, "these batteries are the best that the French make for use aboard submarines."

"True," nodded the fleet commander. "What then?"

"Why, sir, by the use of the cleverest kind of lying that spies can do, Gortchky and his associates have hoodwinked the French and Italian governments into believing that the batteries are to be lawfully used for research purposes, when, as a matter of fact, they are to be used aboard a submarine which the plotters intend to use for destroying a British battleship."

"We will admit, then," said Admiral Timworth, as a poser, "that the plotters have probably gotten into Italy storage batteries that can be used serviceably on a submarine. But where and how can the plotters have obtained the submarine craft itself? Or, if they haven't got it yet, how are they to obtain one? For submarines are not sold in open market, and it would be difficult to steal one."

"I cannot answer that, as yet, sir," Dave admitted gravely.

"And such storage batteries *might* be used for purposes of scientific research," continued the fleet commander.

"Yes, sir; but the habits of the buyers should be considered, should they not? Gortchky and his associates can be hardly believed to be interested in science. On the other hand, they are arch plotters, which would lead us to suppose that they have bought these batteries to further a plot. Outside of scientific work the batteries would not be likely to be used anywhere except on board a submarine. Storage batteries of different size and pattern are used for industrial purposes, but those described in this bill are used on board submarines."

"Your reasoning is plausible, Darrin, and probably correct, too," nodded Admiral Timworth.

"Besides which, sir," Dave pressed home, "if we admit that the plotters have conspired to sink a British battleship at Malta, the easiest way in war-time, when unidentified strangers cannot get aboard a warship, would be to effect the sinking by means of a submarine's torpedo. And, if this be the plan of the plotters, then the crime is likely to be attempted only when there are British and American war craft, and none others, in the Grand Harbor of Malta."

"Yet surely the plotters must know that, between good friends like Britain and America, it would take more than the mere sinking of a British ship to make the English suspect us, as a nation, of being involved in such a dastardly plot."

"Our country couldn't be suspected, as a government or a nation, of being guilty of such a wicked deed," Dave answered. "But Englishmen and Frenchmen might very easily believe that the torpedoing was the work of a group of officers and men in our Navy who hated England enough to strike her below the belt. With the British ship sunk, sir, and with none to suspect but the Americans, there is no telling to what heights British passion might rise. The British are feeling the tension of the great war severely, sir."

"There is one flaw in your reasoning, Mr. Darrin," Admiral Timworth replied. "We will admit that the torpedoing happens at a time when only American and British war craft are visible in Grand Harbor. Why would it not be wholly reasonable for the British to suppose that the torpedoing was the work of a German submarine that had sneaked into the harbor of Malta under the surface of the water?"

"That occurred to me, sir," Dave admitted, "and at first I couldn't find the answer, but at last I did."

"I shall be glad to hear that answer."

"The submarine, let us suppose, sir, discharges

one torpedo with such accuracy as to sink the British battleship. Why could not another torpedo be fired immediately, which would not strike, but would rise to the surface and be afterwards identified when found as an American torpedo? For a torpedo that does not strike and explode can be so adjusted that it will afterwards sink or rise and float. And this torpedo that rises can be of American pattern."

"But where would the plotters secure an American torpedo?" demanded Admiral Timworth.

"The plotters, if they had a secret factory, could make some torpedoes of the American type, provided they had obtained the services of a draftsman and workmen familiar with the American torpedo."

"That could be accomplished, in this wicked old world of ours," nodded Admiral Timworth, after an interval of deep thought. "I won't declare that I think it really has been done. Yet your various reports to me, Mr. Darrin, convince me that plotters really intend to sink a British battleship and lay the blame at our country's door. And such a deed might really provoke English clamor for war with our country."

In the Admiral's quarters a long silence followed.

At length the fleet commander looked up.

"Captain Allen," he asked, "what do you think of Mr. Darrin's surmise?"

"It looks probable to me," said the "Hudson's" commanding officer promptly.

"It looks likely to me, also," sighed Admiral Timworth.

Then the famous old sea-dog brought his clenched fist down on his desk with a bang.

"Malta shall be our next stop," he declared. "We shall see whether any band of plotters can put such a plot through while we are watching! All mankind would shudder at such a tragedy. All the world would side with England and condemn the United States and her Navy! Gentlemen, I now believe that Mr. Darrin has revealed the details of a plan that will be tried. We must prevent it, gentlemen! We shall prevent it — or some of us will lose our lives in the effort to stop it! Darrin, you shall have your chance in helping us to stop it. Mr. Dalzell, you, too, shall have your chance! And now — Malta."

CHAPTER XVIII

SURIGNY'S NEXT MOVE

IN the Grand Harbor, overlooked by the town and fortress of Valetta, on the island of Malta, there lay at anchor the British dreadnaught "Albion," the cruiser "Wrexham" and the gunboat "Spite."

Less than half a mile away lay the American battleships "Hudson" and "Allegheny" and the cruiser "Newton."

It was early evening now. During the day, soon after the arrival of the American craft, the usual visits of courtesy had been exchanged between the two fleets.

Admiral Barkham, of His Majesty's Navy, received a most disagreeable shock while in conference in Admiral Timworth's quarters. In other words, he had been accurately informed of all that was so far known to the American fleet commander.

"But it is impossible," declared Admiral Barkham. "Quite impossible!"

"It would seem so," replied Admiral Timworth. "Yet the outcome will be the best proof in the matter. Sir, with your help, I propose to catch that submarine, should she appear in these waters."

"She will not appear," declared the Englishman. "I am convinced that such a thing is impossible. Only madmen would undertake to accomplish such a horrible thing. True, we have enemies who employ submarines in this war, but they do not dare to use them in attacking battleships. Nor would plotters without the backing of a government dare try it."

Then Admiral Timworth caused Ensigns Darrin and Dalzell to be summoned. They came. Admiral Barkham listened to their story, his gaze all the time fixed on their earnest faces.

It was impossible to doubt the word of two such intelligent young officers. Admiral Barkham found his doubts vanishing. He was prepared to admit that such a crime as he had heard discussed might be in course of planning.

"Of course I know the fellow Gortchky," admitted Admiral Barkham, "and also that troublebreeder, Dalny. Yet this is something amazingly more desperate than they have ever attempted before. I now admit, sir," turning to Admiral Timworth," that there is good reason to suppose that such a plot may be afoot."

"The 'Maine' was sunk in Havana Harbor," rejoined the American Admiral, dryly. "That incident sent two nations to war. Might not something like the 'Maine' affair be attempted here in Valetta Harbor?"

Sitting with bowed head the British admiral looked most uncomfortable.

"At all events," he said, "it is certainly a matter of duty for the officers of both fleets to be on the lookout, and for them to work in concert. Yet I still find it all but impossible to believe what my judgment tells me might be possible."

"You are going to advise the officers of your fleet, then?" asked Admiral Timworth.

"I think so," replied the Englishman slowly.

"In the American fleet," said Admiral Timworth, "very few officers will be told outside of those who are going to be charged with keeping a lookout for the submarine."

At a sign Dave and Dan withdrew, leaving the two fleet commanders in earnest conversation.

"It's hard for an Englishman to conceive of such a crime as being possible, isn't it?" asked Dan, with a melancholy grin.

"Perhaps it's to the honor of his manhood that he cannot believe in it," Dave answered gently, as the chums sat in the latter's quarters.

Dave and Dan had been excused from ship duty on account of other duties that were likely to be assigned to them at any time.

Half an hour after the chums left the Admiral's

"Admiral Barkham listened to their story."

201

quarters an orderly summoned them to Captain Allen's office.

"Both admirals are convinced," said Captain Allen, when Dave and Dan had reported, "that the crime, if it is to be attempted, will be tried at night. As there are still a few hours before dark Admiral Timworth wishes you to take one of the launches and go alongside the British flagship. There will you find three or four young British officers ready to join you. You will all go ashore in Valetta and remain there until nearly dark. You will circulate about the town, as sight-seers usually do. While ashore you will keep your eyes open for glimpses of the Gortchky-Dalny plotters and their subordinates, whom you may find there. Admiral Timworth particularly desires to know whether any of that unsavory crew have reached Malta."

The launch being ready alongside, Dave and Dan, both in uniform, went at once over the side. They were soon alongside the "Albion," and a voice from deck invited them aboard. There the officer of the deck introduced them to four young English officers. Three minutes later the party went aboard the launch, and headed toward shore.

Outside of the forts and garrison buildings the town is a small one, though at this time there were several places of amusement open on two of the principal streets.

Through these places the party strolled, seemingly bent only on having a good time.

"Have you seen any of the bally spies?" murmured one of the young English officers, Whyte by name.

"Not a sign of one," Dave answered in a low tone.

"What if they're not here?" persisted Whyte.

"It may be that none of them will show up at Malta," Darrin answered. "Or it may be that those who do come will come only on that submarine we are looking for."

"I would like to meet one of those plotters," grumbled Dorcliffe, another of the English party and the possessor of a bulky frame and broad shoulders.

"What would you do?" asked Dave smilingly.

"I believe I'd jolly well choke the breath out of him!" asserted Mr. Dorcliffe.

"That would betray the fact that we know the gang and the work that they're planning," Dave returned.

"Would it?" asked Mr. Dorcliffe, looking thoughtful. "Oh, I say! It's bally hard work to contend with such bounders. Why can't all men fight in the open?"

"Real men do," Dave answered. "The fellows we are trying to run down are not real men. Beings who can do wholesale murder for pay are bad beyond the comprehension of honest men."

"But we're not finding any one that we want to see," complained Sutton, another of the English party.

"I didn't expect to find that crew on parade," Dave replied, "and I think it extremely likely that none of them is now in Valetta or on the Island of Malta."

Then all fell silent, for the leaders of the party had turned in at one of the cafés most frequented by visitors.

There were but few people at the tables. Glancing across the room Dave felt a sudden throb of astonishment and disgust.

Hastily rising from a table was a young man who averted his face.

"There's the Count of Surigny!" whispered Dave to Whyte.

An instant later a door at the side of the room closed almost noiselessly, with the young French nobleman on the other side of it.

"Did you see that fellow?" Dave demanded, hoarsely.

"We did," came the acknowledgment of Dave's group.

"That is Surigny," Darrin informed them. "He is the fellow whom I saved from suicide at Monte Carlo, and now he is in the ranks of the men who have planned the worst crime of the twentieth century. Surigny is now where his follies have placed him — associated with the vilest creatures who disgrace the name of Man!"

The party had seated themselves at a table where beverages and refreshments are served. A tireless Italian soprano and a Russian tenor were grinding out some of the stock music of the place. Two dancers were waiting to follow them.

The naval officers looked bored. They were not in this café for pleasure, but strictly for business — that of national honor.

A waiter strolled leisurely into the room, looked about, then approached the table at which the American and English officers were seated. Dropping a towel at Dave's side, the waiter bent over to pick it up, at the same time slyly pressing into Dave's hand a piece of paper.

Holding it under the table and glancing at it, Dave found it carried a brief message in French. Translated, it read:

"For vital reasons, I beg you to follow the waiter, who can be trusted, and come to me at once. Come alone and secretly. Honor depends upon your compliance!   S."

"Surigny!" muttered Ensign Darrin, disgustedly, under his breath. "That impossible scoundrel! He has sold himself to those plotters, and now would betray me. The wretch!"

Yet, after a moment's thought, Dave decided to see the man.

Bending over, Dave whispered to Dan the message contained in the note.

"Are you going?" quivered Dan, his eyes flashing indignation.

"Yes."

"And I?"

"You will remain here, Dan. Tell the others if you can do so without being overheard. Make my excuses after I have left you."

Then, his head erect, his heart pumping indignantly, Dave Darrin rose and sought the waiter, who lingered at the end of the room.

CHAPTER XIX

TRUTH, OR FRENCH ROMANCE

Y OU know what is expected of you?" Dave asked the waiter, in an undertone.

"Yes, Master," replied the man, a Maltese who spoke English with an odd accent.

"Then I will follow you," Darrin added.

At the heels of the waiter Dave went through a narrow corridor, then climbed a flight of stairs.

Pausing before a door, the waiter knocked softly, four times.

"*Entrez, s'il vous plaît*" ("Come in, if you please"), a voice answered.

Throwing open the door, the waiter bowed and swiftly departed.

Ensign Dave Darrin stepped inside, closed the door, and found himself face to face with the Count of Surigny.

That young Frenchman, his face unwontedly pale, searched Dave's face with his eyes.

"You are not glad to see me," he said at last.

"Do I show it?" inquired Darrin, his face without expression.

"You are not glad to see me," Surigny went on rather sadly. "Then it is because you suspect."

"Suspect — what?" Dave demanded, to gain time.

"You know the company that I have been keeping," the young Count continued.

"Has it been the wrong kind of company for a gentleman to keep?" Ensign Darrin asked coldly.

"You know!" cried the Count bitterly.

"Then," asked Dave, "is it indiscreet for me to ask why you have permitted yourself to associate with such company?"

"I doubt if you would believe me," replied Surigny, wincing.

"Is there any good reason why I should believe you?" Dave returned, studying the Frenchman's face.

"Perhaps none so good as the fact that I am a gentleman," the Count of Surigny answered more boldly. "The word of a gentleman is always sacred."

"May I ask to what this talk is leading?"

"I hardly know how to proceed with you," complained the young Frenchman. "Once you did me a great service. You taught me to live and that to die by my own hand was cowardice. Monsieur, you taught me how to be a man."

"And you have remembered the lesson?" Dave inquired, with the same expressionless face.

"I at least know," the Frenchman returned, "that a man should remember and serve his friends."

"Then you have been serving me?"

"I have been working hard, swallowing insult and stifling my sense of decency as far as possible, in order that I might serve you and prove myself worthy to be your friend," replied Surigny, with such earnestness that Darrin now found himself staring in open-eyed astonishment at the young nobleman.

"Perhaps you are going to try to offer me particulars of how you have been preparing to serve me," Dave said with a shrug.

"Monsieur," cried the Frenchman, as if in sudden desperation, "are you prepared to accept my word as you would wish your own to be accepted?"

"Wouldn't that be asking considerable of a comparative stranger?"

"Then answer me upon your own honor, Monsieur Darrin," the Count of Surigny appealed eagerly. "Do you consider me a gentleman or — a rascal?"

Ensign Dave opened his lips, then paused. He was now asked to speak on his own honor.

His pallor giving way to a deep flush, Surigny suddenly opened his lips to speak again.

"Monsieur Darrin," he urged, his voice quavering, "do me the honor to look in my eyes. Study

me from the viewpoint of an honest man. Tell
me whether you will believe what I have to say
to you. Do not be too quick. Take time to
think.''

As Dave found himself gazing into the depths
of the other's eyes, and as he studied that ap-
pealing look, he felt his contempt for Surigny
rapidly slipping away.

''Now, speak!'' begged M. le Comte de Surigny.
''Will you believe what I am about to tell you, as
one man of honor speaks to another?''

For an instant Ensign Dave hesitated. Then
he answered quickly:

''Yes; I will believe you, Monsieur le Comte.''

''In doing so, do you feel the slightest hesitation?''

''Naturally,'' rejoined Darrin, a slight smile
parting his lips, ''I am assailed by some doubts
as to whether I am wise in doing so, but I will believe what you have to say to me. I prefer to
believe you to be, of your own choice, a man of
honor.''

Surigny uttered a cry of delight. Then he went
on:

''Perhaps, Monsieur Darrin, you will even be
willing to set me the example in truthfulness by
telling me whether you know of the plot of those
with whom I have had the shame of being associated.''

"You will doubtless recall, Monsieur le Comte, since it was said only a moment ago, that I promised only to believe what you might have to say to me. I did not promise to tell you anything."

Indeed, at this point, Ensign Dave was perilously near to breaking his word as to believing Surigny. It looked to him as if the Frenchman were "fencing" in order to extract information.

"Well, then," exclaimed Surigny, with a gesture of disappointment, "I will tell you that which I feel I must. Listen, then. With Gortchky, Mender, Dalny and others, I have been engaged in a plan to cause a British warship to be sunk in the harbor yonder, and under circumstances such as to make it appear as the work of you Americans. Did you know that, Monsieur?"

"Go on, "urged Dave Darrin.

"At first," murmured the Count, coming closer, "I believed Gortchky's statement that I was being engaged in secret diplomatic service. When I learned the truth, I was deeply involved with the miserable crew. Also, I was very much in debt, for Gortchky was ever a willing lender.

"There came a day, Monsieur, when there dawned on me the vileness of the wicked plot in which I had become engaged. For a few hours I felt that to destroy myself was the only way in which I could retrieve my honor. But the lesson you had taught served me well in those hours of

need. Then the thought of you, an officer in the
American Navy, brought a new resolve into my
mind. No pledges that I had ignorantly made to
such scoundrels could bind me. I was not their
slave. Pledges to do anything that could bring
dishonor upon one are not binding on a man of
honor. I did not even feel a sense of debt to
Gortchky, for he had used the money with evil
intentions. From the moment of these realiza-
tions I had but one object in view. I would go
on taking such money as I needed, and with no
thought of the debt; and I would serve these
monsters with such seeming fidelity that I could
at last find my way open to serving *you* fully,
Monsieur Darrin. I pause for an instant. Do
you believe all that I have just told you, my
friend?"

"Yes," answered Dave. The next second he
caught himself wondering if, through that "yes,"
he had unintentionally lied.

CHAPTER XX

THE ALLIES CLEAR FOR ACTION

I LEFT Naples for this island on an east-bound liner," continued the Count of Surigny. "Not until within an hour of sailing did I know the whole of the terrible story that now spoils my sleep at night and haunts me by day. Monsieur Darrin, if you have scented any dreadful plot, at least I do not believe you know just what it is."

Once more the young Frenchman paused. Dave, however, having regained his expressionless facial appearance, only said:

"Go on, Monsieur le Comte."

"Then I have but to tell you what the plot is," resumed Surigny. "Gortchky, Mender, Dalny and others knew that the American fleet would stop at Malta, because American fleets in these waters always do stop at Malta. They knew also that a British fleet often remains here for months at a time. So these arch scoundrels knew to a certainty that the 'Hudson' of your Navy would be here in due course of time. In a word, every plan has been made for sinking a British battleship here at Malta under circumstances which will make it appear to be plainly the work of a group of American naval men."

Darrin, still silent, steadily eyed the Frenchman.

"You do not start!" uttered Surigny, in amazement. "Then it must be because you already know of the plot!"

"Go on, please," urged Dave quietly.

"The plan must have been made long ago," the Frenchman continued, "for, before August, 1914, before the great war started, though just when I do not know, Gortchky and the others, or their superiors, had a submarine completed at Trieste. It was supposed to be a secret order placed for the Turkish government. The craft was not a large one. Gortchky and some associates took the submarine out for trial themselves. Days later they returned, reporting that the underseas craft had foundered, but that they had escaped to land in a collapsible boat. Most of the payments on the submersible had already been made. Gortchky paid the balance without protest, and the matter was all but forgotten.

"I do not know what reason Gortchky had given the builder, if indeed he offered any explanation, but the tubes in the submarine had been made of the right dimensions and fitted with the right mechanism to fire the American torpedo. And a man whom I judge to have been a German spy in America before the war — a German who had served as draftsman in the employ of an American munitions firm — was at Trieste to furnish the design for both the torpedo tubes and for the four American torpedoes that the Trieste firm also supplied.

"You will have divined, of course, Monsieur Darrin," Surigny continued, "that the submarine was not lost, but concealed at a point somewhere along the shores of the Mediterranean until wanted. So far ahead do some enemies plot! Where the submarine has remained during the interval I do not know, but I do know that, submerged only deep enough for concealment, she has been towed to these waters recently by relays of fishing boats manned by Maltese traitors to Britain. Ah, those rascally Maltese! They know no country and they laugh at patriotism. They worship only the dollar, and are ever ready to sell themselves! And the submarine will endeavor to sink the British battleship to-night!"

"To-night!" gasped Darrin, now thoroughly aroused.

"To-night," Surigny nodded, sadly, his face ghastly pale. "Even the yacht that carries the plotters is here."

"These are hardly the times," Dave remarked, "when it would seem to any naval commander a plausible thing for a yacht to cruise in the submarine-infested Mediterranean. And, if the plotters are using and directing the movements of a yacht, I am unable to see how they could obtain clearance papers from any port."

"Oh, the yacht's sailing papers are correct," Surigny declared, eagerly. "The yacht has Russian registry and is supposed to be sold to Japanese buyers to be put in trade between the United States and Japan, carrying materials from which the Japanese make Russian munitions of war. So you will see how plausible it is to be engaged in transferring a Russian yacht to Japanese registry at this time."

"Humph!" grunted Darrin. "It seems a stupid thing, indeed, for any Japanese shipping firm to buy a low, narrow craft, like the typical yacht, to convert her into a freighter."

"Ah, but the yacht is neither low nor narrow," replied Surigny. "She is a craft of some three thousand tons, broad of beam and with plenty of freeboard."

"What flag does she fly?" Dave asked.

"That I do not know," was the Count's answer. "It may be that she does not fly any. Two of her passengers are reported to be a Russian prince and a Japanese marquis. But Monsieur Mender is not a Russian at all, and no more a prince than he is a Russian. As for the Japanese, he is merely a Filipino, once a mess attendant in your Navy, and now a deserter, for he hates your country."

"When will the yacht reach these waters?" Dave inquired.

"As I have said, she is here already, or as near as she will come," the Frenchman continued. "At noon she was at anchorage in the channel between the islands of Comino and Gozo. It is known as the North Channel."

"I know the spot," said Dave, nodding. "Comino is the little island that is used as a quarantine station. Monsieur le Comte, do you know anything more, of importance, that you have not already told me?"

"Monsieur Darrin, I believe that nothing of importance has been left out of my narrative. But you believe me? You will now accept my hand?"

"Yes," Dave burst out, extending his hand almost impulsively. M. le Comte Surigny seized it delightedly.

"Ah, it is good, it is grand!" cried the young Frenchman, "after such associates as I have had for weeks, to find myself again fit for the confidence and the friendship of a gentleman!"

"But what will become of you?" asked Dave, a feeling of regret suddenly assailing him. "What will become of you, my dear Surigny? Is it

likely that the plotters, if they be foiled, will
suspect you? Is it likely that they would seek
your life as a forfeit?"

"What is my life?" laughed the Frenchman
gayly. "I have never valued it highly, but now,
when I have won back my self-respect, a blow
in the dark would be but a mark of honor. If
they wish to kill me, let them. It would be a
glorious death, in the cause of honor!"

Dave glanced out of the window, then gave a
start of alarm.

"Time is passing," he murmured. "I must take
my information where it will be of the most
service. And you, Surigny, may I take the liberty,
without waiting to ask our Admiral's leave, of
inviting you to accept the hospitality of the flagship? Will you come on board with me?"

"Afterward," replied the Frenchman. "Afterward, when the truth of what I have told you is
recognized."

"Where will you stay for the present, then?"

"Where I am now," smiled the Count.

Dave took one long step forward, again gripping
Count Surigny's right hand with both his own
hands.

"Surigny, I am under more obligations than I
can ever repay. Few men with the instinct of
a gentleman could have endured, for weeks,
having to associate with and serve such rascals

as this grewsome crew. You have, indeed,
proved yourself noble, and I deeply regret that
I have ever allowed myself to distrust and dislike
you."

"Let us say no more," begged the Count.
"After the chase is over — and may you win the
game — you will find me here, reveling in the
thought that I have been able to warn you so
completely."

Had it not been that he again remembered how
late it was growing, Ensign Darrin would have
remained longer with this now bright-faced
Frenchman. As it was, Dave tore himself away
from Surigny, and lost no time in rejoining his
party below.

As Dave stepped to the table, Lieutenant
Whyte, of the British Navy, raised his eyebrows
in slight interrogation. None spoke.

"I don't know," smiled Darrin, "how it goes
with you gentlemen of England, but I am sure
Dalzell will agree with me that it is time to get
back to our ship."

"It is," Dalzell affirmed, taking the cue.

The score was settled, after which the party
left the hotel. Dave stepped to Whyte's side.
Through the streets of the little town the party
passed quickly by twos, gayly chatting. Once
they were clear of the streets and near the mole
Dave began:

"Mr. Whyte, the moment for action is at hand. Surigny sent for me, and I believe he has told me the truth. He felt under obligations, and, when invited, joined the international plotters in order to find out how he could serve me. He has told me that a yacht bearing the supervising plotters is now anchored in North Channel, and that the submarine is concealed somewhere under neighboring waters. It is the intention of the plotters to attempt to sink one of your ships to-night."

"Do you believe the fellow?" demanded Whyte in a shocked tone.

"At first I found it hard to believe him," Dave admitted, "but now I believe that he told me the truth."

"And if he has not?" questioned the British officer.

"In any event, Whyte, the yacht must be watched. However, your Admiral Barkham will have to decide what action shall be taken."

"Do you know whether others of the crew, besides Surigny, are in Valetta?" Whyte asked.

"I did not ask Surigny," Dave rejoined. "Indeed, it is not important to know. What we must do is to catch the submarine; the conspirators may wait for subsequent overhauling."

At Darrin's signal the launch from the flagship promptly put off. Darrin ordered that the

English officers be put aboard their own ship first. As the launch drew alongside the "Albion" Dave added:

"Mr. Whyte, I shall wait until you ascertain whether your Admiral has any message to send to Admiral Timworth. That, of course, would be after hearing your report."

For ten minutes the "Hudson's" launch lay alongside the "Albion." Then Mr. Whyte appeared, coming nimbly down the gangway and stepping into the launch.

"With Admiral Barkham's compliments, I am to carry a message to Admiral Timworth," Whyte announced. "I am also to inquire whether your Captain desires a conference with Admiral Timworth before I deliver my message."

Dave conducted the English officer aboard the American flagship. Captain Allen soon received them. He heard Ensign Darrin's report, then telephoned to Admiral Timworth for permission to bring to his quarters the English admiral's representative, together with his own youngest officers.

Admiral Timworth received them, listening attentively to the report that Dave had to make of his conversation with the Count of Surigny.

"Do you believe that the Frenchman was telling the truth?" the fleet commander inquired. Dave answered in the affirmative.

"Does your message from Admiral Barkham concern the Frenchman's report?" inquired Admiral Timworth, turning to Whyte, who had kept modestly in the background.

"It does, sir," Lieutenant Whyte answered, stepping forward. "Admiral Barkham's compliments, sir, and he has used the wireless to the quarantine station on Comino Island. Such a yacht as the Count of Surigny described is at anchor in North Channel, and is reported to have a Russian prince and a Japanese nobleman on board. So Admiral Barkham gives at least that much credence to the Frenchman's story."

Whyte paused a moment, that Admiral Timworth might speak, if he chose, then continued:

"Admiral Barkham imagines, sir, that you would like to have a share in searching the yacht and in guarding against submarine attack. To that end, sir, he signaled to the military governor at Malta and secured the latter's assent to a plan of having the American naval forces co-operate with us in running down the plot."

"Of course we shall be glad to aid," declared Admiral Timworth, heartily, "and we are much complimented over being invited to help you in British waters."

CHAPTER XXI

MAKING STERN WORK OF IT

LIEUTENANT WHYTE then unfolded, briefly, the plan of Admiral Barkham for procedure against the yacht and the submarine. To these plans Admiral Timworth quickly agreed.

"We have four large launches on the flagship," the fleet commander stated. "Three of these shall be put over the side, officered and manned and ready for instant service."

"Admiral Barkham also suggests, sir, that, during the night, the officers in command of your launches run without lights, when possible, for secrecy," Whyte continued.

"How many launches will Admiral Barkham put in service?" Admiral Timworth inquired.

"Three, sir," responded Whyte.

"Who will be the ranking officer in your fleet of launches?"

"I believe I am to be, sir," Lieutenant Whyte replied, bowing.

"Very good," nodded Admiral Timworth. "It would not be courteous, in British waters, Mr.

Whyte, for me to appoint an officer who would
rank yourself, so I shall ask Captain Allen to
designate Ensign Darrin as ranking officer in
our launch fleet. Ensign Dalzell will naturally
command another of the launches. Who will
command the third, Captain?"

"Ensign Phillips," replied Captain Allen.

The courtesy of appointing an ensign to head
the American launch fleet lay in the fact that
an ensign is one grade lower in the service than
a junior lieutenant. When naval forces of different nations act together the ranking officer,
no matter what country he represents, is in
command. Had Admiral Timworth put his
launch fleet in charge of a lieutenant commander,
for instance, then the British launches, too,
would have been under the command of the
American officer. As it was, Lieutenant Whyte
would be ranking and commanding officer in
the combined launch fleet. This was both right
and courteous, as Malta is an English possession,
and the waters near by are British waters.

Plans were briefly discussed, yet with the
thoroughness that is given to all naval operations.
Lieutenant Whyte departed, and Ensign Phillips
was sent for. Admiral Timworth and Captain
Allen charged the young officers with their
duties, upon the successful performance of which
so much depended.

"Remember, gentlemen," was Captain Allen's final word, "that, in line with what the Admiral has stated, you are merely to co-operate with, and act under the orders of, the British ranking officer. Yet, if occasion arise, you will display all needed initiative in attaining the objective, which is the capture of the scoundrelly plotters and the seizure of the submarine before it can work any mischief. You will even sink the submarine by ramming, if no other course be open to stop her wicked work."

Each of the flagship's launches was equipped with a searchlight. While the council was going on in the Admiral's quarters the electricians of the ship were busy overhauling these searchlights and making sure that all were in perfect working order.

From the British flagship came a prearranged signal to the effect that Lieutenant Whyte was about to put off.

Dave's launch crew comprised, besides machinists and the quartermaster, twenty-four sailors and eight marines. A one-pound rapid-fire gun was mounted in the bow, and a machine gun amidships.

"Send your men over the side, Ensign Darrin," Captain Allen ordered, as he took Dave's hand. "Go, and keep in mind, every second, how much your work means to-night."

"Aye, aye, sir," Dave answered.

When the word was passed Dave's launch party was marched out on deck and sent down over the side. Dave Darrin took his place in the stern, standing by to receive any further instructions that might be shouted down to him. "Cast off and clear!" called down the executive officer.

Dan Dalzell, whose launch party was not to clear until a later hour, waved a hand at his chum. Dave waved back in general salute.

At the same time Lieutenant Whyte put off from the "Albion" and sped onward to meet the American craft.

"We are to sail in company to North Channel," called Whyte.

"Very good, sir," Dave answered, saluting.

With three hundred feet of clear water between them, the launches moved rapidly along.

The distance to the middle of North Channel was about fifteen miles. Time and speed had been so calculated that the yacht should not be able to sight them by daylight. After dark the two launches were to maneuver more closely together, and Whyte, who knew the North Channel, was to be pilot for both craft until it came time to use their searchlights.

Over in the west the sun went down. Darkness soon came on. Neither launch displayed even running lights. One had a sense of groping his way, yet the launches dashed along at full speed.

Dave Darrin was now in the bow, with the signalman at his side, who would turn on the searchlight when so ordered. With his night glasses at his eyes, Ensign Dave could tell when the British launch veered sharply to port or starboard, and thus was able to steer his own course accordingly.

Twelve minutes later a brief ray shot from the Englishman's searchlight. It was the signal.

"Turn on your light," Dave ordered to the man at his side. "Swing it until you pick up the North Channel. Then pick up and hold a yacht —"

Ensign Darrin followed with the best description he had of the strange yacht.

Less than a minute later the lights on both navy launches had picked up the strange yacht, well over in the Channel. Dave studied her through his glass.

"That's the craft," Darrin muttered to himself. "My, but she looks her part! While she isn't large for a freighter, she's well calculated for that class of work."

"Your best speed ahead, sir!" shouted Whyte, through a megaphone. "Board the yacht on her starboard quarter. Quick work, sir!"

"Very good, sir!" Dave called back.

Then he stepped swiftly amidships to the engineers.

"Get every inch of speed to be had out of the engines, my man."

Next, to the helmsman:

"Quartermaster, steer straight ahead and make that yacht's starboard quarter!"

As Dave turned, he found his own face within three inches of Seaman Runkle's glowing countenance.

"Runkle," Dave smiled, "we are fond of the Englishmen. Their commanding officer called for our best speed, and we're going to show it."

"Aye, aye, sir!" grinned Runkle. "When any foreigner asks for the best we have in speed, he's likely to see it, sir."

Already the "Hudson's" launch had drawn smartly ahead of the British craft, and the distance between them grew steadily, though the Englishman was doing his best to keep up in the race.

Under the yacht's stern dashed the launch, and brought up smartly under the starboard quarter, laying alongside.

"Hullo, there! Vat you call wrong?" demanded a voice in broken English from the yacht's rail.

"Naval party coming aboard, sir," Dave responded courteously. "Take a line!"

"I vill not!" came the defiant answer.

"All the same, then," Dave answered lightly. "Bow, there! Make fast with grapple. Stern, do the same!"

Two lines were thrown, each with a grappling hook on the end. These caught on the yacht's rail. Three or four sailormen, one after the other, climbed the grappling lines. Two rope ladders were swiftly rigged over the side, by the Americans on the yacht's deck. Dave Darrin was quickly on board, with twenty of his seamen and all his marines, by the time that the English launch rounded in alongside the port quarter.

"You? Vat you mean?" demanded a short, swarthy-faced man, evidently captain of the yacht, as he peered at Dave's party. "You are American sailors!"

"Right," Darrin nodded.

"And dese are British vaters!"

"No matter," Dave smiled back at the blustering fellow. "Here come the Englishmen."

For he had sent four of his men to catch and make fast the lines from the British launch, and now the British jack-tars, taking their beating in the race good-humoredly, were piling on board.

"Captain," cried Lieutenant Whyte, striding forward, "I represent Admiral Barkham, ranking officer of His Majesty's Navy in these waters.

I have the Admiral's orders to search this craft."

"You search him for vat, sir?" demanded the skipper.

"My orders are secret, sir. The search will begin at once. Ensign Darrin, if you will leave your marines to hold the deck, we will use all our seamen and yours below."

"Very good, sir," Dave replied, saluting. "You do not wish any one allowed to leave the yacht, do you, Lieutenant?"

"Not without my permission or yours, Ensign."

Dave accordingly gave the order to the corporal in charge of his marine party.

In another minute American and English tars were swarming below decks on the yacht.

On deck and in the wheel house Darrin had not seen more than four men of the yacht's crew, besides the skipper.

"There do not seem to be any men below," Dave muttered, as he explored the yacht between decks. "I wonder if that skipper gets along with four deck hands in addition to his engine-room and steward forces."

His men in squads, under petty officers, worked rapidly. Dave Darrin moved more slowly, passing on into the dining cabin and the social hall of the yacht, which were below decks.

Adjoining the social hall were several cabins.

Dave threw open the doors of the first few he came to, finding in them no signs of occupation.

Then a steward, smiling and bowing, appeared and asked him in French:

"Do you seek any one here?"

"You have a Prince aboard?" Dave asked.

"Even so."

"And a Japanese nobleman?"

"We have."

"I wish to see them."

"Both are resting at present," the steward expostulated.

"I must see them immediately," Dave insisted.

"It is hardly possible, sir," protested the steward. "It is not to be expected that I can disturb such august guests."

"Steward, do you wish me to summon my men and have these cabin doors battered down?"

"Do not do that!" urged the steward in alarm. "Wait! I have pass-keys. Which would you see first?"

"The Prince, by all means."

"I will admit you to his room, Monsieur, and next silently slip away. But be good enough to let the Prince believe that he left his door unlocked. This way, monsieur."

Finishing his whispered speech, the steward glided ahead. He unlocked a cabin door, opening it but a crack. Dave stepped softly inside.

Instantly the door was pulled shut and locked.

Through transoms on opposite sides of the cabin Mender and Dalny showed their evil faces, as each trained on the young naval officer an ugly-looking naval revolver.

CHAPTER XXII

AFTER THE PEST OF THE SEAS

"MAKE a sound, and you feed the fishes, my fine young naval dandy!" hissed Dalny.

"Pooh!" retorted Dave, contemptuously. "Order your steward to unlock that door, or I shall be put to the trouble of smashing it down with my shoulder."

"And be shot in the back while you are doing it," jeered Mender.

"I haven't had the honor of meeting you before, but I take it that you are the bogus Russian Prince," laughed Dave. "Just now, though, you look much more like an apprentice to the Black Hand."

"You should be saying your prayers, instead of talking impudence," sneered Dalny.

"As for this cardboard Prince, words fail me," mocked Dave, still speaking in French, "but as for you, Dalny, I have already tested your courage, and know it to be worthless. You are a coward, and would not dare to use that revolver, knowing, as you must, that my men are aboard and would tear you to pieces. Go ahead and shoot, if you dare. I am going to break my way out of this cabin, and then I shall arrest both of you."

"Is there no way of compromising?" begged Dalny, his evil face paling. "In exchange for your life, Monsieur Darrin, can you not offer us a chance for escape?"

"One brave man down!" laughed Ensign Dave. "That was spoken like the coward that you are, Dalny."

Darrin turned to break down the door. He knew that he was taking chances, for the sham Prince might be a man cast in a braver mould than Dalny, and, in his desperation, might shoot at the back that Dave so recklessly presented.

At the third lunge from Darrin's sturdy shoulder the door snapped open at the lock. The young naval officer stepped out into the social hall. There was no sign of the steward.

"Seaman here!" Dave bawled lustily. He was obliged to repeat the summons twice before a hearty "Aye, aye, sir!" was heard in the distance.

Then Jack Runkle showed his jovial face at the top of the companionway. Catching sight of his officer, Runkle bounded down the steps and came up on a run, saluting.

"Runkle, go to the corporal of marines

and ask him to send two men here. Then stand
by."

"Aye, aye, sir."

Runkle was off like a shot on his errand and
soon returned with two marines.

"Now, men," Dave directed, pointing to the
doors, "batter them down. That door, first."

As the men aligned themselves for the assault,
Darrin, mindful that the sham Prince was armed
and might prove ugly, stood by with his revolver
drawn.

Bang! crash! The door was down.

"It will be wise to surrender to superior force,"
Darrin called sternly. "We shall shoot to kill at
any sign of resistance."

As the words were uttered in French the marines
did not understand, but they advanced unhesi-
tatingly on Mender, disarmed him and led him
outside the room.

"Take care of him, Runkle," ordered Dave.
"Now, marines, that other door!"

Down came the barrier, and Dalny, shaking
and white, was brought out to keep Mender
company.

"Break down every door that's locked," was
Darrin's next order.

Within five minutes a little, quaking brown
man was secured and led out. All the locked
cabins had now been entered.

"You're the Japanese marquis, are you?"
Dave jeered. "Do you find, Marquis, that it
pays any better than being a Filipino mess
attendant?"

The Filipino hung his head without answering.

"Take these prisoners to the corporal of marines,
and ask him to iron them and watch them closely,"
Dave directed. "Runkle, do you know where
Lieutenant Whyte is?"

"In the hold, sir, or was." ·

"Follow me, then, and we'll see if we can find
him."

Down in the main cargo hold forward, Dave
and Runkle came upon Whyte and a party of
English and American sailormen.

"Ah, there you are, Mr. Darrin," called Whyte.
"We've been making a jolly big search through
the hold, but, except for ship's supplies, it appears
to contain nothing very interesting. However,
we shall have time to examine it further later
on. And you?"

"I have three prisoners," Dave explained, and
told who and what they were.

"Take them with you, Ensign, if you have
room on your launch," Whyte directed. "I
will now take my men above and post a guard,
so that you may withdraw your own guard
and get under way at once."

"We have done well so far," Dave answered,

as he gripped the English officer's hand. "I pray that we may be permitted to do as well all through the night."

Runkle was sent through the craft to recall all of the American sailors.

When Dave reached the deck he found that the entire crew of the yacht, including the engine-room force and the stewards, had been rounded up and driven to the deck.

"Over the side," directed Darrin, as his men, recalled, gathered near him. He followed, but went over last of all. Orders for casting off and shoving clear were instantly given.

"Keep the engines up to their best performance all the way," was Dave's order. "Boatswain's mate, watch sharp for the courses, as I may change frequently."

"Aye, aye, sir."

Heading out of North Channel, Dave drove back for Valetta, keeping about a mile off the coast.

After making a few knots, he came abreast of another British launch that lay further to seaward. With lantern signals the Englishman asked:

"Is the submarine supposed to be loose?"

"Yes," Dave had his signalman reply.

"Where?"

"Don't know."

"I'm here to warn incoming ships against entering Grand Harbor to-night," the Englishman wound up. "Are you seeking the submarine?"

"Yes," Dave had flashed back.

"Good luck to you!" came heartily from the English launch.

"Thank you," was Darrin's final response.

The searchlight of Dave's launch was swinging busily from side to side, searching every bit of the water's surface that could be reached.

"If the submarine comes up, Runkle, you may be the first to sight her," Dave smiled to that seaman, who stood beside him.

"Aye, aye, sir; if I sight that craft I won't be mean enough to keep my news to myself."

"I wonder where Dalzell is," thought Dave. "What is he doing in this night's work?"

As for Ensign Dave, his every nerve was keyed to its highest pitch. Outwardly he was wholly calm, but he felt all the responsibility that rested upon him to-night, as did every other officer who commanded a launch from either fleet.

Searchlight and naked vision were not enough. Almost constantly Darrin had his night glass at his eyes.

Suddenly, as the light shifted over the water, Dave thought he caught sight of something unusual.

"Steady with that light there, signalman," he

commanded suddenly. "Back slowly to port with the beam."

Darrin forced himself to be calm.

"Steady," he called, again. "Hold the light on anything you see, signalman."

"Aye, aye, sir; I *do* see something," replied the man who was manipulating the searchlight.

That he did see the mysterious something was proved by the manner in which he kept the light upon it.

That on which Darrin now trained his night glass was a marked rippling on the water, half a mile away, and farther seaward. A landsman would have missed it altogether. Yet that rippling on the sea's surface was clearly different from the motion of the water near by.

"It might be a school of large fish," Dave mused aloud, in Runkle's hearing, "though at night they are likely to rest. Runkle, and you, men, keep your eyes peeled to see if you can make out fish leaping out of the water."

The ripple continued, unbroken at any point. Moreover, it moved at uniform speed, and in a line nearly parallel with the coast.

Gradually the launch gained on that ripple. Dave could not turn his fascinated gaze away from the sight.

"I think I know what that is, sir," broke in Seaman Runkle, after three minutes of watching.

"I am sure that I *do*, Runkle," Dave Darrin returned. "It's a submarine, for some reason just barely submerged. That line of ripple is the wake left by her periscope."

As if to confirm the young naval officer's words, the ripple parted. As the line on the water broke, the periscope came fully into view, and the turret showed above water, continuing to rise until the deck was awash.

"There's the pest of the seas!" cried an excited voice.

Every man on the launch was now straining his eyes for a better look at the submarine, barely a quarter of a mile away.

CHAPTER XXIII

THE PUZZLE OF THE DEEP

COXSWAIN!" shouted Dave.

"Aye, aye, sir."

"Send up three blue rockets!"

"Aye, aye, sir."

One after another the rockets ascended, bursting high overhead and slowly falling.

From Grand Harbor, several miles distant, a rocket ascended and burst, showing red.

Darrin's signal had been seen and answered.
Both fleets now knew that one of the launches
had sighted the submarine craft. The three blue
rockets had been the signal agreed upon in advance. Runkle was at the gun. Ensign Darrin
gave him the range.

"I wish we had a four-inch gun in the bow,"
Dave muttered wistfully, "but we'll have to do
the best we can with the one-pounder. Ready!
Fire!"

Even before the command to fire had been
uttered the craft ahead had begun to submerge.

As the brisk, snappy report of the little piece
sounded, and a faint puff of smoke left her muzzle,
Runkle's head bobbed up to watch the result of
his shot.

"Forward of her turret by about a foot!"
Runkle muttered in disgusted criticism of his
own shooting.

A sailor had thrown the breech open, while a
second swabbed the bore through and the first
fitted in a fresh shell, closing the breech with a
snap.

Runkle seemed to sight and fire almost in the
same instant, and, as before, straightened up
to watch the accuracy of his shot by the splash
of water on the other side of the craft. The
launch's searchlight held a steady glare on the
mark.

"Nearer by a few inches, sir," Runkle called over his shoulder while the men with him swabbed and loaded. Again Runkle fired.

"The shell must have passed aft of the turret by about six inches," remarked Darrin, catching through his glass a glimpse of the splash of water where the little shell struck the waves.

"I'll do better, or drown myself, sir," growled Runkle.

"Quick! She is submerging rapidly," commanded Darrin.

Bang! An instant after the report a smothered exclamation came from the unhappy gunner. The submarine had safely submerged. Not even her periscope was above water now.

"If the turret had been four inches nearer the sky you'd have put it out of commission," declared Ensign Darrin.

"Rotten work," growled Runkle in disgust.

"It's night shooting, my man," Dave answered. "Good work just the same."

Runkle had an excellent gunnery record, and Darrin did not like to see that fine fellow fretting when he had done his best. None the less it was highly important to send that submarine to the bottom and quickly at that.

"We've got to go by bubbles, now," Darrin declared. "She isn't likely to show her eye again."

Had he gotten the launch close enough to observe the bubbles it is possible that the young ensign could have followed the enemy trail. Twice or thrice Dave believed that he had picked up glimpses of bubbles with the searchlight, but at last, with a sigh, he gave orders to shut off speed and drift.   Inaction became wellnigh insupportable after a few moments and Darrin called for slow speed ahead.

"There she is again," he cried. "There's her periscope.   The scoundrel is standing out to sea."

Over the starboard quarter the searchlight signals of two other launches were observed.

"What's taking place?" came the signaled question from one.

"Fired a few shots at a vanishing turret, but missed," Dave ordered signaled back. "Enemy standing out to sea. Am following."

"Will follow also," flashed back the answer.

"And one of their gunners will bag the game at the first chance," groaned Runkle. "The jinx is sitting tight on my chest to-night!"

"It might be, if there were any such animal as a jinx," laughed Darrin. "Your missing was just plain bad luck, Runkle. Your shooting was good."

"The periscope is being pulled inboard, sir," called one of the seamen who stood by with Runkle.

"I see it. There she goes, under again," Dave answered.

The Navy launch was dashing full speed ahead. But with no clue to follow, Darrin passed some anxious seconds. Should he follow on the course he had been taking, or should he shut off speed? In the dark there was a good chance that the submarine commander, if so minded, would be able to double and head back for shore.

Land lights were still visible from his position. Dave turned to estimate their distance.

"About six knots off shore," he concluded, half aloud.

"Sir?" questioned the corporal of marines, thinking the ensign was addressing him.

"I was just telling myself that we're about six knots off shore."

"Yes, sir," replied the corporal, saluting.

"Listen to me, you men who are near enough to hear. Your understanding of what is in my mind may help you the better to work with me on this job. Two launches are keeping with us, over the starboard, and I judge the nearer one to be about four knots off. Coxswain, use the lantern signal and ask who commands."

Soon Hardy discovered that, in order to make his signal visible at that distance, he would have to stand higher. Springing to the forward deck his signal was instantly understood on the other craft.

Dave, who had jumped up beside him, read the answer:

"Ensign Dalzell."

"I was sure of it," Dave smiled. "Coxswain, order number 2 launch to come up on parallel course, standing off half-mile to starboard of us."

"Order understood," was flashed back from Dalzell's launch.

Bit by bit Dan overhauled, at last taking the position indicated. Darrin's launch was moving at slow speed now, for he did not care to run out of sight of land, thus leaving the way clear for the submarine to double on him and put back toward Grand Harbor.

"Why doesn't the fellow take a chance on torpedoing us?" was signaled from Dalzell's launch.

"He has only three," was Darrin's reply.

That was brief, but Danny Grin understood, as Dave had intended he should, that the submarine was believed to be equipped with only three torpedoes. Evidently the enemy still hoped for a chance to sink a British battleship.

Suddenly he discovered that for which he sought, and in the same instant a seaman called, as the rays of the searchlight shifted:

"Periscope two points off the port bow, sir."

"Right!" clicked Ensign Darrin.

"May I fire, sir?" begged Runkle, bending over his piece.

"Yes, try it. Pretty long shot, though."

Before Runkle could aim and discharge his piece a swift, red flash shot from the bow of the number 2 launch commanded by Danny Grin. Runkle fired a second later, but the periscope still stood as if mocking the eager gunners.

"I'm glad somebody else missed," growled Runkle, who was becoming exasperated. He was doing himself injustice, though, for each time he had fired, his mark, considering the distance, had been small, and the searchlight was no peer of daylight in aiding a gunner.

Ensign Darrin admitted to himself that he was stumped. He ordered the course changed, with speed ahead, his purpose being to scan the water for the bubbled trail left by the underseas craft. But by the time that he judged himself to be going over the recently observed position of the submersible the searchlight revealed no bubbles.

The third launch now coming in close, Dave, by signal, ordered Ensign Sutton of the British forces to go slowly inshore. He too was to watch for bubbles, as well as to be alert for a re-appearance of the enemy craft.

The longer the suspense lasted, the more uneasy Darrin became.

"There she is, sir!" called a low but penetrating

voice from the stern watch. "Three points off the stern to port, sir."

So quickly did the helmsman bring the launch about that she heeled and shipped a volume of water. Darrin, as he leaped upon the forward deck, ordered the sailor manning the searchlight to shut off.

"Don't turn it on again without orders. I believe I can follow the pest with my glass if she will only keep her conning tower above water. Signalman, send my order to the other launches not to use their searchlights without first asking permission."

By this time Darrin, standing on the forward deck, had the submarine's turret, or as much of it as showed, in the field of his night-glass.

Not more than a foot of it showed above water, and, even through the glass, at a distance of nearly half a mile, it would hardly have been discernible without the aid of the searchlight, had it not been for the white wake left by the turret in its course through the water.

"May I try a shot now, sir?" begged Runkle. "I'm certain I can hit the turret this time."

"If you could do it surely, you'd be the best shot in the Navy," smiled Darrin. "I'm not going to use the searchlight unless I have to, and it would be almost impossible to make a hit in the dark without it. The pest is headed shoreward, and I want to creep up close from the rear, if possible."

Dissatisfied, Runkle none the less saluted and turned back to his gun.

"Keep a close sight on the sneak," Dave called after him. "When you hear me call 'Ready!' you will complete your aim and fire without further orders."

An order transmitted to the man standing by the engine sent the launch plunging ahead at increased speed.

Of a sudden the pursuit assumed a new aspect. The submarine suddenly veered around to port, and then headed straight toward the launch.

"Now's our chance!" glowed a seaman, excitedly.

"Yes," retorted another strained voice. "Our chance for death!"

The same thought came into the minds of many on the launch. The submarine, it seemed, was about to discharge a torpedo at the pursuer.

"Starboard!" commanded Darrin. "Keep her bow to port of us!"

Seaman Jack Runkle strained his ears for the solitary word from Ensign Darrin that would be so welcome.

"Will he ever give that order?" fumed the impatient sailor at the breech of the one-pounder.

CHAPTER XXIV

CONCLUSION

"STAND by, gunner!" warned Darrin.

"Aye, aye, sir!" came from the man at the one-pounder.

The crew had ceased to be on tension, for it had dawned upon them that, as the two craft were approaching each other almost head on, there was hardly a chance that a torpedo could be made to register.

"Ready!" Darrin ordered.

There was a sharp bark from the throat of the one-pounder. Smash! A cheer went up from the watching seamen. The shot hit the mark. But the two men with Runkle were cleaning and loading for still another shot at the conning tower.

"Any more, sir?" inquired Runkle, with a grin, after firing and landing a second shot in the submarine's superstructure.

"Not unless ordered," Darrin answered, crisply. "If that fellow dives now he'll go below and stay there for good."

Instead of diving, however, the top of the submarine's conning tower was seen to rise higher and higher above the water.

"She's rising, but she's lost her steerage way, sir," announced the corporal of marines.

"The helmsman was undoubtedly killed by the first or second shot," suggested Dave. "It looks as if the survivors mean to surrender, but we'll watch out for tricks."

He gave the order for slow speed ahead, soon reducing it to mere headway.

"Marines prepare to board," ordered the ensign, as the launch came up close to the now unmanageable submarine, whose deck showed a bit more than awash.

It called for fine work on the part of the quartermaster to set his launch alongside without crushing it.

Gauging closely with his eye, Ensign Darrin called out:

"Ready to board! Board!"

Making the first leap himself, Dave landed on both feet on the slippery deck of the under-sea boat, the marines following eagerly and quickly.

"Lay off and wait!" Dave called back to the quartermaster. Then he stepped closer to the conning tower, through which two holes had been drilled by the two registering one-pound shells.

"Open up, you fellows down there!" Dave called, briskly. "And don't attempt any tricks."

Inside he heard shuffling movements, but there was no evidence of intent to obey his order. So he called again, but this time spoke in French, believing that order might be more easily understood by those inside the submarine.

"Don't shoot! I'll come up and open," answered a voice in broken French, strongly tinged with Maltese accent.

After a few moments the hatch was raised. Then, one after another, eight or ten of Darrin's crew went below.

"No more men below," ordered Dave, who then followed his men in.

It was a miserable spectacle that met his eyes. A heavy body lay face downward in a pool of blood on the steel deck.

"Who was this?" demanded Dave, of the other four men who crouched to one side in fear and trembling.

"Gortchky," answered one of the quartette sullenly.

There could be little danger of mistaking the dead man. Though no feature of the face had been preserved, every line in that odious body stood out clearly in Dave Darrin's mind. It was, indeed, all that was left of Emil Gortchky. Mr. Green Hat would never again steal the secrets of nor plot trouble between nations!

"An able man, even if a wicked one," said Dave slowly, uncovering in the presence of Death.

The body of Emil Gortchky was allowed to re-

main where it lay. The other four men of the
submarine crew, one of whom was proved later
to be an expert submarine commander and a
deserter from the Swedish navy, were taken up
to the platform deck, and thence transferred to
the launch, where they were put beside Mender,
Dalny, the badly-scared Filipino, and the other
prisoners removed from the yacht.

In the meantime Dan Dalzell had ranged up
alongside, followed by Sutton of His Majesty's
Navy. Both of these young officers went aboard
the submarine and below deck for a look.

Rocket signals had informed those on anxious
watch in Grand Harbor of the capture of the submarine. Congratulations had been signaled back.

Just as the dawn broke, watchers in the waters
near Valetta saw Dave Darrin's launch enter the
harbor, the submarine limping along in tow.

Early as the hour was, a band was lined up on
the quarter deck of the "Albion." When Darrin's
boat was within six cable-lengths, the band broke
out exultingly into the strains of "See the Con-
quering Hero Comes!"

Probably no naval officer so young as Dave Darrin had ever been so signally honored by a foreign
naval commander as was Dave Darrin then.

The submarine was anchored on a spot indicated
by the port authorities of Valetta. Then Dave
Darrin shaped his course for the "Hudson."

From hundreds of men, lined up on the decks of the flagship, rose lusty cheers.

"Bully boy, Darrin!" shouted a group of officers from the quarter-deck.

"Ensign Darrin," cried Admiral Timworth, striding forth from his quarters and grasping the young ensign by the hand. "I offer you my heartiest congratulations! For reward you shall have anything within my power to grant."

"Sir, I know what I want most at present," Ensign Darrin replied, gravely.

"What?" asked the Admiral, quickly.

"A nap, a bath, clean clothing and a breakfast, sir."

"But later on, Mr. Darrin?"

"At Port Said, sir, I shall ask Captain Allen to grant me, if it does not interfere with duty, three days ashore to meet my wife, whom I expect to find there when the fleet arrives."

For, as readers of the Boys of the Army Series are aware, Dave and his High School sweetheart, Belle Meade, were wedded immediately at the end of some border troubles in which Dave and Dick Prescott were involved on the Mexican border.

Despite, or perhaps on account of, the stirring experiences through which he had passed, Darrin was asleep five minutes after his head touched the pillow.

Danny Grin, who had been in only at the finish, lay awake for an hour before slumber visited him.

All that was left of Emil Gortchky was dropped into an unmarked, unhonored grave at Malta. Mender, Dalny and the Filipino were condemned by a British court-martial to be shot, a sentence that was soon after carried out.

As for the master and crew of the yacht, they persisted to the end in strenuously denying any guilty knowledge of the real intentions of the plotters. They escaped the death sentence, but, as their conduct was none the less of a guilty nature, the master of the yacht received a sentence of twenty years in prison, while his subordinate officers and the members of the crew were imprisoned for ten years each.

On information supplied to the Italian government Countess Ripoli was arrested. She was not an Italian woman, but had married an Italian nobleman who had died, after which she had turned to spy work. She was locked up and held for trial at Rome, but died of a fever before the day of her trial arrived.

The minor spies and the thugs employed by Gortchky and Dalny, unless they have since fallen into trouble with their own local police, have, of course, gone unpunished.

George Cushing, the secret service agent, is now on duty in the Panama Canal Zone.

M. le Comte de Surigny was a happy man when Dave visited him ashore on the day following the capture of the submarine. Surigny is now in Paris, the valued friend of a noted advocate, in whose offices he is studying law. An inheritance of comfortable proportions has since come to the Count, but he has determined upon a career of hard work. He is a strong, fine character in these days, and is proving, to the full, the manhood that Dave Darrin awakened in him.

The fleet remained a week at Port Said, Egypt. Dave had three happy days ashore with Mrs. Belle Darrin, and Danny Grin was often to be found in their company.

Jack Runkle received his promised rating, becoming a boatswain's mate. He is now industriously climbing the ladder of promotion.

It is reluctantly, indeed, that we take leave of Dave Darrin in this volume, but we shall meet him and Danny Grin again, and very soon, in the pages of the next volume of this series, which will be published under the title, "DAVE DARRIN'S SOUTH AMERICAN CRUISE; or, Two Innocent Young Naval Tools of an Infamous Conspiracy." In this absorbing story Dave Darrin and Dan Dalzell are shown at their best as faithful and loyal officers of Uncle Sam's Navy.

THE END